End of the Race

END OF THE
RACE

DEAN HUGHES

Atheneum 1993
New York
Maxwell Macmillan Canada
Toronto
Maxwell Macmillan International
New York Oxford Singapore Sydney

Atheneum
Macmillan Publishing Company
866 Third Avenue
New York, NY 10022

Maxwell Macmillan Canada, Inc.
1200 Eglinton Avenue East
Suite 200
Don Mills, Ontario M3C 3N1

Macmillan Publishing Company is part of the Maxwell
Communication Group of Companies.

First edition
Printed in the United States of America
10 9 8 7 6 5 4 3 2 1
Library of Congress Cataloging-in-Publication Data
Hughes, Dean, date.
End of the race / by Dean Hughes—1st ed.
p.   cm.
Summary: Two twelve-year-old boys, one black and one
white, train for and compete in the 400-meter race, but find it
hard to become friends because of racial differences and their
fathers' past relationship.
ISBN 0–689–31779–4
[1. Track and field—Fiction. 2. Race relations—Fiction.
3. Friendship—Fiction.] I. Title.
PZ7.H87312En   1993
[Fic]—dc20   92–37747

For Allen and Margaret Ramsey

C h a p t e r   1

Jared Olsen took a deep breath. He pressed his left foot against one starting block and reached back with his right leg to the other. He rested his weight on his knees, raised up and brushed the little chunks of rubber, from the track, off his hands. Then he leaned forward again, placed his hands, with his fingers stretched wide, just behind the starting line, and looked down the track.

Jared concentrated on the track and shut everything else out. One hundred meters. Nothing between him and the finish line—just that clear path between those white lines.

These were tryouts, and Jared wanted to make the summer track team as one of the sprinters. Another group had already run, and Jared knew that two of those guys were fast. He had to win this heat, and he had to have a good time.

Someone to his right was still moving, taking his time. Jared wished he hadn't gotten ready so quickly. The waiting was making him tense. He could feel the tightness spreading out from his chest and into his arms.

The seconds pounded away like heartbeats. The white lines shimmered in the June heat and seemed to squeeze in on each other.

"Seh-uuuhhhht."

Jared extended his legs and let his body rise. Then he held—tight—his legs cocked, his eyes locked on the track.

A clock in his head counted, while his legs and arms quivered to release. But the timer kept holding and Jared thought he would explode before . . .

Bang!

He burst from the blocks, drove his legs for a few hard, quick steps, and let his body straighten. Then he stretched into full strides.

And he was out in front. He couldn't see anyone on either side. All he saw were those lines—that simple lane to the finish.

He felt his spikes biting, springing . . . *pam, pam, pam* . . . as though he were hardly touching the track.

And then at fifty, maybe sixty meters, he felt them coming—a runner on his left, and another one way outside on the right. He tried to push harder, drive his arms, strain for all the speed he could get.

But it wasn't there. Those blurs on either side of him were moving up, almost even.

At about eighty meters he knew the guy on his left had him, but he pushed all the harder. And now his legs felt heavy, as though his spikes were sticking in the track.

He leaned at the finish, and he held one guy off.

But the runner on his left had him by a step. He was older, a tall kid named Shawn Morgan who would be an eighth grader in the fall.

Jared had thought he was faster than Morgan— and he *had* been for eighty meters—but his start was always the best part of his race.

He jogged on ahead and stopped. Staring up at the nearby mountains, he wiped the sweat from his forehead and ran his hand over his crew-cut hair.

He hated that frustrating feeling that he had given all his effort but just hadn't been fast enough. He couldn't will himself to be faster, couldn't practice speed. There was simply no excuse to give his dad and his big brother. He would have to tell them he hadn't made it.

"Hey, Jared."

Jared looked over at Davin Carter, a guy he knew from school. They weren't close friends, but Jared knew him better than most of the kids who were trying out.

"I came in the same as you did—second in my heat."

Jared nodded. "Yeah, I know."

"I can't figure it out. I thought us black guys were always supposed to be faster."

Jared laughed but he looked away. Davin was always saying things like that, but Jared never knew how to react.

"Neither one of us will be sprinting," Davin said. "The coach said he's only using two in our age group, and I'm pretty sure Morgan beat my time."

Davin didn't sound as though he cared all that much. But then, he always sounded that way. He was one of the best athletes at Jared's school, where the two of them had just finished sixth grade. But he never seemed to go all out—at sports or at anything else.

"I *know* I won't be," Jared said between breaths, and he tried hard to hide his disappointment. He wanted to sound as easy about the whole thing as Davin.

He decided to jog a slow lap. He told himself he needed to cool down, but he really wanted to get away from everyone.

All the way around the track he talked to himself. He didn't have to be *too* disappointed. He was only twelve, and he was running in the twelve-and-thirteen age category. The two sprinters who had won the heats were thirteen. Besides, this was summer track—an Athletic Congress team. No one would be cut. Almost a hundred kids were going out for the team, maybe a few more of them boys than girls. But that was for all five age categories. Jared had counted eleven boys in his age group. Jared would just have to settle for something other than sprints to run.

But thoughts of Kent, his older brother, hovered over Jared like ghosts. Kent, at the same age, had been the fastest kid in the whole area. He had never lost a hundred-meter race until he got to the state championships in his junior year of high school. Then he finished second in the state.

Jared saw that Coach Heywood was calling everyone together, so he picked up his speed. He was one of the last to get to the gathering on the infield grass. Jared sat down on the grass next to Davin.

4

"Okay, kids," Coach Heywood said, "I've got the teams pretty well set, at least for the first meet. No team scores are kept at these early meets. The emphasis is on letting you develop your talents in the areas where you can do the best. So that's what I've been trying to find out. I'd like to see some of you qualify for the state championships later this summer."

Coach Heywood was a tall black man with rich brown skin. His chest and shoulder muscles were cut clean under his gray T-shirt. But he bulged a little around the middle, and his hair was thinning in front. What Jared liked was the way he talked to the kids. He wasn't one of those barking coaches Jared had sometimes had in Little League or in recreation-league basketball. He spoke softly, and he already knew almost everyone's name. Jared's dad had told Jared that Coach Heywood had been a star athlete in Ogden, years ago. He still lived in Ogden, but he had been coaching at the high school in Wasatch for several years now.

"We have some good distance runners," the coach said. "You kids who trained all spring for junior high and high school track are in good shape, and there's a bunch of you who like to run those longer races. Where some of you could do well, I think, is in the four hundred and eight hundred. Those are the distances no one likes to run."

Jared knew why. They were killer races.

Coach Heywood, beginning with the sixteen- and seventeen-year-old group, told the runners which races he wanted them to enter, and he tried to get more kids involved in some of the field events.

Jared was wondering what he ought to tell his dad. He had imagined himself saying, "Dad, I'm going to run the hundred meters. I beat out all the older guys." And he had pictured his dad, beaming and pleased. Of course, he had really known that it probably wouldn't happen.

"In the twelve- and thirteen-year-old group, I've got Russell and Morgan in the hundred and two hundred," the coach was saying. "The next fastest were Carter and Olsen, so they'll join Russell and Morgan in the four-by-one-hundred relay."

Yes! That was good. It was something Jared could tell his dad. It made him a sprinter. Maybe before the season was over he could beat out . . .

"Carter and Olsen, I'm also going to have you run the four hundred."

Jared's head popped up. The coach must have seen his disappointment—or shock. Jared was never one who could hide his feelings. He was a light-haired, fair-skinned boy who blushed easily, and his eyes had a way of widening into huge circles when he was surprised.

But Davin was the one who said, "The *four hundred?* Oh, Coach, don't do that to me."

Davin laughed, but Jared saw nothing funny in the idea. Kent had told him that he had only run the four hundred twice, but he had vomited afterward, both times.

The coach cocked his head to one side and shrugged his shoulders as if to say, "Hey, I'm sorry." But what he said was, "Look, in time you two might turn out to be sprinters. But both of you have long legs and good strides. I have to believe this will be the best race for you, not just this year but when you get older."

Jared was feeling sick. He knew the coach was trying to find a good event for him. But the four hundred? It was almost a sprint—but all the way around the track. Jared didn't want to run that far, that fast. In fact, he didn't think he could.

Coach Heywood smiled and said gently, almost apologetically, "Well, maybe it'll make men out of you."

"It's gonna *kill* me," Davin said, but he didn't really seem all that upset. He reached over and gave Jared a little shove on the shoulder. "At least I only have to run against a slow white boy," he said.

Everyone laughed. Especially Davin.

The team was almost all white. But then, most of the people in Wasatch, outside Ogden, Utah, were white. In Ogden there were a fair number of minorities, especially Hispanics, but Wasatch was a suburb, set in the foothills of the mountains. Davin and his little sister were the only two blacks in the elementary school, and they hadn't moved to Wasatch until the middle of this school year.

Jared laughed too, but he didn't like Davin's joking about something like that. Having never spent much time around black people, he felt a little uncomfortable, not sure what he should say, or whether he should even mention race. He wouldn't dare joke with Davin the same way.

Jared wasn't sure the coach liked the joke either. There was one other black guy on the team, an eighth grade hurdler named J. C. Cotler. Jared saw him look at Davin and laugh. "That's right," he said. But the coach, who normally smiled easily, didn't react. Jared thought he saw his eyes narrow a little, just the hint of a scowl, as though he wanted to say to Davin, "Let's not get that kind of stuff started." He chose to ignore it instead.

"Okay, do any of you have anything else you would like to try to compete in? We still could use some more help in the field events."

Jared raised his hand, and when the coach called on him he said, "I'd like to try the long jump."

"Yeah, me too," Davin said.

"Okay, that's good," Coach Heywood said. "I've got Russell and Morgan down for long jump, but you two guys work on it too."

Jared hoped he could do well enough to be at least third. But he suspected Davin might be better.

The coach ended the meeting by asking them all to jog a slow mile before they left. He promised that he was going to start demanding a lot more of them in workouts now that tryouts were finished.

"We only have two and a half weeks until our first meet," he told the team. "That doesn't give us much time. You kids will have to do what I ask of you—and go all out. A lot of you have just finished track at school, so you won't have it so bad. But you younger kids have a lot of work to do." And then the smile again. "Especially Jared and Davin."

Shawn Morgan had been sitting near Jared. As he stood up he looked down and said, "I don't envy you two."

And a big eighth grader named Evan Garner, a shot-putter, said, "Man, the four hundred would *kill* me."

A tall girl who ran distances—Becky something—laughed at Evan and told him, "It would kill you to run far enough to throw a javelin."

"I know," Evan said, laughing with his big, heavy voice. "I tried it once and decided I'd stick with the shot put."

"So how are you going to run a mile?" another one of the girls asked him.

"*Very* slowly," Evan answered. "*Verrrrrrry* slowly." He walked onto the track and began an exaggerated little bounce of a stride that got him almost nowhere.

Jared walked to the track too and started his own slow jog. He found himself alone. He really didn't know many of the kids on the team except for some who lived in his neighborhood, and none of those were his age. His best friend, a boy named Nick Clifford, had left for the whole summer. His father was a professor, the same as Jared's dad, at nearby Weber State University. He had gotten a study grant to go to England, so Nick would be spending the summer doing all sorts of exciting stuff. Jared was stuck home alone.

As Jared thought about that, the loneliness really hit him. The one thing he had hoped for—the chance to run the hundred meters—was gone now, and what did he have left?

The four hundred.

As Jared jogged around the first turn he thought again of his dad and brother. He knew exactly how they would react. They would tell him he had done well for a twelve-year-old, that the four hundred was a great race, and they were proud of him. But he would also hear the faint strain in their voices. That would be the disappointment that they couldn't quite hide—because now the truth would be out. Jared wasn't going to be as fast as Kent.

Chapter 2

When Jared finished running his mile he walked another lap, and then he did the cool-down exercises that the coach had taught everyone. Most of the runners didn't bother with the exercises; they just cleared out.

The summer heat was coming on, so workouts started at eight o'clock every morning. It was a little after eleven now. Jared was not really sure what he was going to do. He had imagined the day, but only up to the point where he called his dad and told him that he had won a spot as a sprinter. Now he didn't think he would call.

As he walked through the stadium gate he saw Davin unlocking his bike. "Hey, Davin, I didn't know you had a mountain bike," Jared said. "I've got one too."

"I just got mine," Davin said. "I was thinking I might start riding up into the hills around here."

Jared hesitated, but then he asked, "Do you want to go for a ride now?"

"Uh . . . yeah. I guess." Davin hesitated too, as

though he were trying to think of some excuse not to go. "I could go for a little while."

"I know some trails," Jared said. "We don't have to do anything too hard at first."

"Hey, don't worry. I can keep up with *you*."

Davin was joking; Jared knew that. But again Jared felt awkward.

Jared strapped his duffel bag on the back of his bike. He rode on ahead, and Davin followed. He pumped uphill a couple of blocks on pavement and then onto a dirt road into the foothills.

Jared pushed pretty hard, and he didn't gear down much. He had spent a lot of time on his bike, and after that comment he wanted to work Davin a little. Maybe it wouldn't be so easy for Davin to keep up as he thought.

Davin stayed pretty close, however, and Jared kept pressing. They continued that way for maybe a mile up the trail. Then Jared slowed and finally stopped at a little pond. He was breathing hard, but at least Davin had dropped back a little.

"Hey," Davin said, "I *told* you I could stay with you." He drew in a long breath. "I just didn't say how long." Sweat was glistening on his forehead and on his upper lip.

Jared laughed and then leaned down and rested his forearms across his bike's handlebars. His legs were tingling from all the work they had done that morning. "Yeah, well, I was wearing out too," he said.

When Jared finally stood up straight again he saw that Davin was looking out at the pond. Davin was a guy who looked "in command." His features seemed carved, like a statue's, the bones of his face firm and strong. And yet, his style never quite fit those looks. From the little Jared knew of him, Davin seemed quick to make fun of things. And his deep brown eyes had a way of sliding off to one side, as though they weren't quite in sync with those solid cheekbones—as though the real Davin were peeking out from behind a mask.

"I didn't even know this pond was up here," Davin said.

"Not many do. But I come up here all the time."

The whole pond was not more than a couple hundred feet across. The water was silver in the morning light, the same color as the hazy sky. Low oak brush grew down to the shore on three sides, casting shadows on the silver, turning the surface black near the banks. On the near side, where the trail passed by, a little grove of quaking aspen dropped mottled patterns of light and shade on the brown June grass.

"Can you swim in there?"

"Yeah. It's not very deep, and the bottom is sort of rocky along this side, but Nick and I swam in it a couple of times. The water is still really cold this time of year."

"Nick Clifford?"

"Yeah."

"Why didn't he go out for the track team?"

"He's in England. His dad's doing research over there."

"You two are pretty tight, aren't you?"

"Yeah."

Davin looked back at the water. Jared had the

strange impression that Davin looked a little disappointed, or at least more thoughtful than usual.

"I'd rather swim in a pool," he said. "We used to swim in a pond sometimes when I lived in Oregon. I hated it when I'd step down and the mud would ooze up between my toes." He laughed, but he kept looking out at the water.

"Why did you move here?" Jared asked. "Did your dad get transferred or something?"

"No. My dad grew up around here—over in Ogden. And my grandma still lives there. Dad always tells me, 'Well, Davin, I need to be closer to my mother, with her health the way it is. And it *is* my home—whether you like it here or not.' "

Davin had deepened his voice and made it sound big and hollow, apparently to imitate his father. He always did that sort of thing at school when he wanted to make fun of a teacher. He could catch the exact way that Mr. Marchant held his chin, and the gritty sound of his voice.

"Don't you like it here?"

Davin seemed surprised. His eyes, for once, focused in on Jared. "Do *you*?"

"Yeah. I guess. It's the only place I've lived."

Davin used the deep voice again. "It *is* my home," he said.

"So you liked Oregon better?" Jared set his bike on its side and then walked over and sat down on the grass, near the pond.

"Yeah. A lot better."

"What was so different?" Jared asked, looking back.

Davin took a long look at Jared, as though he

were deciding whether he would answer. Finally he looked away and shrugged. "A lot of things."

Jared didn't understand that. Why didn't Davin just tell him? "Were you in a big city or—"

"A suburb of Portland."

Jared took a rather deep breath, thought for a moment, but then took a chance. "Were there more black people up there?"

"Sure."

Davin looked at Jared straight on. But Jared couldn't tell what he was thinking, so he took another chance. "Is it hard to live here—where almost everyone's white?"

"Why should it be?" Davin asked, and now Jared saw a challenge in his eyes.

Jared ducked his head and said, "I don't know. I just thought . . . it might be."

Silence followed, and Jared wished he hadn't said anything. But then Davin surprised him. His voice softened, and he said, "Yeah. Sure it's hard. I never know . . . what to think."

Jared wasn't sure what Davin meant, but he wasn't about to ask any more questions. He let it go.

Davin set his bike down. "If we bike up here every day," he said, "that might be a good way to get in shape."

Jared was glad for the change of subject. "We can go a lot higher," he said. "There's a really tough trail, clear up to the top of this first hill."

"Hill? It looks like a mountain to me."

"Yeah, well, it's a hard climb."

Davin looked at the rounded peak above them. It was probably a couple thousand feet above the little pond. "Are you kidding?" he said. "Have you ridden up there?"

"Not really. I tried. Nick and I did. But we ended up pushing our bikes after a while, and finally we just dumped the bikes and hiked the rest of the way."

"Forget that," Davin said. "I don't want to be a distance runner. I just want to *survive* the four hundred until the coach lets me be a sprinter."

"Yeah, me too. Kent, my big brother, ran the sprints. He says that's the only way to go. You walk off the track, take a few breaths, and you're okay. But the four hundred is supposed to be *bad*."

"Is your brother pretty fast?"

"Yeah. At least he *was*." Jared reached back and braced himself with both arms. He bent his bare legs to keep them out of the prickly grass. "He took second at state in the hundred when he was a junior. He started on the football team that year too—at wide receiver. He was going to be this giant star. And then when he was a senior—last fall—he tore up his knee. He had surgery and missed the rest of the season. He still ran this spring. But he didn't do very well."

"So is he going to play college football or anything?" Davin walked closer to the pond, but he didn't sit down.

"No. He wanted to. That's all he ever used to talk about. My dad and him had their minds made up that he was going to make it to the NFL. But now Kent's just going to go to college and not play sports. I guess he's going to be a doctor. But I'm not sure that's what he really wants. It's just something else Dad thinks he would be good at."

Davin finally sat down on a rock that wasn't really flat enough to look comfortable. He was still wearing the bright red tank top that the coach had handed out at practice that morning. He looked down on Jared. For the first time it occurred to Jared what a strange term for a person "black" is. Davin was dark brown, the color of a chestnut, and there were shades in his skin. His temples and cheeks were light, his shoulders darker. It seemed strange to Jared that he had never noticed that before.

"So what does your dad say to *you?*" Davin asked.

"About what?"

"Doesn't he want you to play in the NFL or something like that?" Davin smiled, and his eyes angled past Jared. It was a look that Jared didn't know how to read, as though Davin were making fun of him.

"I don't know. I'm not as good at sports as Kent. Dad always says he doesn't want to pressure me. But when I do play, and mess up, it's like I'm letting him down. And Kent's even worse. He comes to my games and tries to coach me. If I can't do what he tells me, he thinks I'm not trying. Everything was always easy for him."

"Hey, man, I'd trade you—any day." Davin's smile disappeared.

"What do you mean?"

"My dad was the state champ in the hundred *and* two hundred. And he was a big-deal running back on the football team—all-world, or something. According to him, he was the greatest athlete who ever lived. And he's not going to let me forget it." Davin's jaw pushed forward, and his voice deepened again. " 'Davin, you've got the ability; you just don't put out the effort. You've grown up with everything handed to you. You'd be better off if you had to work for things, the way I did.' "

Jared laughed. "Does he really sound like that?"

"Oh, yeah."

"You make him sound like an actor—like in a Shakespeare play or something."

"That's exactly what he'd want you to think too. He took lessons to learn to talk like that."

"Why?"

Davin looked down at the ground. "You gotta know my dad," he said. "He's a businessman. His *image* means everything to him."

"The worst thing about my dad," Jared said, "is that he never comes right out and tells me what he thinks. He'll say, 'Jared, that's fine—if you did your best. I just hope you're being honest with yourself about your effort.' "

Jared had tried to sound like his dad, serious and sort of overly kind, but he knew that he had gotten it a little wrong. Dad really never sounded quite that phony.

"So was your dad a big athlete too?" Davin asked.

"Sort of. He played football, but I don't think he was any kind of star. He ran the hurdles in track. He always tells how he made it to the state finals and then hit the first hurdle and almost fell. So he finished last." Jared tried again to imitate his father. " 'I'll always wonder. I might have won, with the great start I had. But that's how life is.' "

Davin laughed, but he said, "Hey, at least he admits he lost. To hear my dad tell it, he never lost a race in his life. One time I told him, 'I checked in the book of world records, Dad, and you don't have any of 'em. So somebody must have been faster than you.'"

"What did he say?"

"Oooh-oooh. I'm not going to say anything like that to him again. I thought he was going to rip my head off."

All the same, Davin laughed with delight, as though it were a favorite memory. Jared thought maybe his own dad wasn't so bad after all. Really, his dad was a good guy most of the time. Jared felt a little guilty about making fun of him, even though he was tired of living up to Kent. Jared's mom always told him just to be himself. But it wasn't that easy.

"With me," Jared said, "sports are only part of it. Kent *and* Lori—my big sister—do really well in school too. So I have to come home with good grades—or get 'the look.'"

"Oh, *yes*! I know the look. My dad wants me to be the first black president, I think. He's always saying that if I'll work hard enough he can send me to Harvard—or anywhere I want to go. 'You can write your own ticket, son.'" Again the deep voice. "'When I was your age, I would have given *anything* to have a chance like that.'"

"It sounds like your dad has a lot of money if he can afford all that."

"Oh, yeah, my daddy's rich. He had a company in Oregon—a cleaning service. Ten zillion employees all cleaning office buildings at night. Then he sold it all. Now he owns a whole bunch of those little gas station stores and some other stuff. He flies all over the place. And oh man does he love it. He's a big shot, and he knows it."

"My dad's a chemistry professor. I think the big thing to him is that his own dad didn't even go to high school, and now he has his doctor's degree. He does some work for some companies, besides teaching, and my mom is a high school English teacher. So we do okay. But we're not rich."

"You po' little white boy."

Jared half laughed. He told himself that Davin didn't really mean anything by stuff like that. It was just his way of kidding around. But it still made Jared uncomfortable.

Davin bent, picked up a rock, and then sidearmed it out across the water. It only skipped once and then sank in the silver water. "Are you going to let the coach push you into running the four hundred?" he asked.

"I guess so." Jared let his breath blow out. He hated the thought of it.

"Me too. There's no way my dad is going to let me quit the team—which is what I'd rather do."

"My dad would *let* me. He'd just be . . . disappointed."

Davin nodded. "If that's all I'd get, I'd quit. Right now. But I'm not given any choices."

Jared reached down and picked up a flat stone. He bent way to the side, still sitting, and with a quick flip of his wrist tossed it over the surface of the water. It hit and skipped five or six times before it slipped under. The rings it left behind expanded in interlaced circles, rippling the silvery water.

"Hey, good one," Davin said. "I gotta top that." He began looking for a rock. But as he searched, he said, "We gotta get in *good* shape for the four hundred—or we'll die."

"I know. But I'm not going to kill myself. I'd rather bike to get in shape than do that much running."

Davin had found a rock now, and he was concentrating. He made a hard throw, low and sharp, but the stone skipped only three times before it caught in the water and went down.

"Oh, man, that was a good rock. I should have had you with that one." He began looking again. "I don't really care what we do," he said. "But I don't want to barf every time I race. So I might as well get in shape. Of course, I'll never run fast enough . . ."

The seriousness was back, and this time, when the two looked at each other straight on, some understanding seemed to pass between them. It occurred to Jared that maybe the two of them could become friends.

Chapter 3

The next day at practice Coach Heywood had Davin and Jared run the four hundred for the first time. He put them in with some older guys who normally ran the eight hundred or fifteen hundred. "Set a nice easy pace. These guys are just getting into this," the coach told a kid named Will Belliston, who was a ninth grader.

Will nodded and smiled. He was a thin, long-legged boy with curly red hair. People said the guy could run forever. Jared was not at all sure that he would follow the coach's instructions.

The coach turned to Jared and Davin. "Just try to stay with him, but don't kill yourself this first time." His little smile appeared and he added, "You can do that later."

Jared's stomach suddenly felt empty, fuzzy, the way it felt when he was getting carsick. He didn't even like to jog laps. How was he going to *run* that far?

But he walked to the starting line with the other

runners—Will and three older guys. No one used blocks. They stood at the line and the coach gave them a "get set . . . *go!*"

Will burst ahead of the others, digging pretty hard. Jared's nervousness exploded into energy. He caught Will after a few meters and ran alongside him. He told himself he was running too fast, but it seemed an easy enough pace compared to the sprints.

As the runners reached the first corner, Jared tucked in behind Will. He concentrated on Will's pace. Jared soon realized that he had to take more strides, but he tried to stretch out and glide.

Through the corner Jared felt strong. He knew he was holding plenty back. He should be all right.

As the runners came out of the turn, the rushing sound of the air disappeared. Jared felt as though he were coasting, with the wind at his back. This wasn't bad. Behind him he heard the breathing and the soft thump of spikes on the rubber track. He wondered where Davin was.

Midway down the back stretch Jared was starting to work for air, and his legs were losing their snap. His impulse was to let up, but he told himself he could stay with Will.

As they reached the second curve, however, Jared's legs really started to slow. Pain was working its way into his chest, under his collarbone, and shooting out to his sides. A burning had begun in his lungs. He didn't know how much worse it might get.

On around the curve. But everything was changing. He was going into himself now, forgetting the others. Something was happening to his body. He felt a strange vibration, the beginning of a numbness that spread from his chest and shoulders into his brain. He couldn't get enough air.

He was still trying to float—just glide—but his spikes pounded harder against the track. Will was pulling away.

Maybe fifty meters to go. Jared tried to drive his arms the way the coach had told him to do, but he was slowing more all the time. The wind was in his face again, whistling in his ears, resisting, sapping his power.

He drove his arms all the harder, tried to dig down, but his legs felt like they were turning into tree stumps. A sickening metallic taste was choking him. His chest was heaving, aching, and the numbness was taking over. Even his vision was blurring.

Will was long gone, and now someone else was passing him. "Good-bye," the kid said, an older boy named Mike Gibby. Then the other two older boys went by.

Jared didn't care. He was still trying, but he couldn't get his knees up, couldn't do any more than push his feet ahead. His thighs were burning. He thought of quitting, but he told himself he had to finish.

He expected Davin to pass him any second. But he didn't care. He didn't care about anything but getting this over, ending the sickness, and then he was going to quit track. He would never do this again.

Coach Heywood yelled, "Come on, boys, push it on in. Relax. Don't tighten up."

Jared wanted to scream at him to shut up. It had been a rotten trick to stick him in with Belliston. The pace had been too fast. What was the coach trying to do?

Jared's legs almost quit the last few strides, and he limped across the line. Davin crossed at about the same time. The two of them staggered ahead for a few steps, and then they both dropped on the track. Jared rolled onto his back and clapped his hand over his eyes to block out the harsh sunlight. He was sure he was going to vomit; he wanted to get away from everyone. Still, he lay on the track and sucked for air. A terrific pain was grabbing at his ribs and shoulder blades.

"I won't run that race," Davin gasped. "I'm quitting."

"Me too," Jared said as soon as he could get enough breath to speak.

The coach was there now, kneeling beside them. "Will set a pretty good pace," he said. "So now you know what you're up against. It's a tough race, and the only thing that makes it easier is to work your tails off. But for your first try, you did all right. Once you can keep that early pace all the way to the end, you'll be competitive."

Jared didn't tell him yet. He didn't have enough breath. But he was definitely quitting.

"You need to get up now and jog a slow lap—so you don't stiffen up."

Jared did get up, but he walked to the grass and then dropped to his knees and bent forward, his head on his arms. He didn't want to vomit—not where everyone could see him. He would get away somewhere to do that. Right now he was still trying to get air, still waiting for the numbness to stop buzzing through his head.

"Give yourself another minute or so, and then jog a lap," the coach said.

"I can't run that far," Davin choked out. He was still lying on the track. "I don't want to do the four hundred."

Jared heard the older boys laugh. He glanced up and saw that they were already jogging away.

Coach Heywood laughed too, but gently. "Hey, I don't blame you," he said. "Nobody *likes* the race. But you guys are going to know you've accomplished something by the end of the summer."

Jared didn't care about any of that. He just wanted to get his breath back, then vomit, then get away.

Some of the older girls were getting ready to run next. The one named Becky walked over to Jared. "It always feels like you're going to die when you first finish. But you feel better after a few minutes—and the better shape you're in, the faster you recover."

Jared looked up at her and nodded, but he wasn't sure he was buying it. All the same—and to his surprise—he did begin to feel better after a couple of minutes. He finally sat up, even though he stayed on his knees. Davin had gotten up, but he was bent forward with his hands on his thighs.

"Okay, guys, jog a lap, nice and slow," Coach Heywood said.

Jared waited. He watched Davin, who finally looked back at him. He was obviously waiting to see what Jared would do.

"Go ahead," the coach urged.

And so Jared got up and walked onto the track. He stopped and took a couple of long breaths and began a little trot. He could have walked twice as fast. When he didn't feel Davin coming with him he looked back. Davin was still standing, looking at him. Jared stopped. Maybe both of them *would* get the nerve to quit.

"Davin, you've got to push yourself a little," the coach said. "I won't ask too much of you, but you've gotta be willing to pay your dues if you want to be a runner."

Davin's eyes dropped, as though he were saying, "Sorry, Jared, I guess I've got to do this." And he began a little trot of his own. Jared waited for him, and then the two jogged off together, very slowly.

"I can't quit," Davin said. He took a breath. "My dad would never let me get away with it."

Jared knew he couldn't quit either. By now he was admitting it. But he didn't say that. "Do you need to puke?" he asked.

"I guess not. I thought I was going to at first."

Jared nodded. It was true. The nausea really was passing away, even if the pain in his legs was not. But they jogged the rest of the way around the track.

After that, Coach Heywood told them to work on their long jumping. But that was a joke. Neither one had enough spring left to run the approach, let alone jump. So mostly they stood around and watched other kids jump.

Coach Heywood paid no attention, or at least he didn't say anything. At the end of practice he asked everyone to jog a mile again. Jared and Davin were two of the last ones to finish their four laps, and they were really dragging by the end.

The coach called all the kids together before he let

them leave. "All right," he told them, "in the next couple of weeks we have to build your stamina. We're going to be running into the hills some, and we're going to push you a little. So come tomorrow morning ready to work." He reviewed some of the training rules, talked to them about their eating, and then sent them home.

Davin and Jared walked out of the stadium together. They had talked about trying to ride up the trail today. But now Davin said, "I can't ride my bike uphill. I'll be lucky to get home."

"Same here," Jared told him.

"If you want, we can ride down to my place," Davin said. "I've got a swimming pool."

"I'm too tired to swim."

"Yeah, well, me too. We can get something to drink anyway."

"Uh . . . yeah. Okay." For some reason, Jared felt strange about doing that. But he did feel a closer connection to Davin now.

The boys followed a winding hillside street for half a mile. Davin's house was only five or six blocks from Jared's, but it was farther up the mountain, in a cul-de-sac where all the houses looked like mansions.

By the time they got there, Jared's legs were clutching in little spasms. The boys dropped their bikes on the front lawn, near the driveway, and hobbled through the garage—a three-car garage—to get inside. Jared took a good look at a dark green Mercedes parked in the first stall.

"That's my dad's new car," Davin said. "He must be home. I think he's leaving town today."

The boys entered through a little utility room and then walked down a hall. Jared could see that the house was new, and everything was beautiful. The carpets were light, almost white. Jared looked into the living room and saw the fancy gray-blue drapes and the huge front window that offered a view of the whole valley.

Davin took Jared to the kitchen. "What do you want to drink?" Davin asked.

"Is that you, Davin?" someone called. Jared liked the sound of her voice, smooth and low, and maybe a little southern.

"Yeah, Mom." Davin walked on into the kitchen, and Jared followed. It was a big, bright room, with light oak cabinets and lots of windows.

Davin opened the refrigerator at about the same time that his mother walked into the kitchen. "Oh, hi," she said when she saw Jared.

"Mom, this is Jared Olsen. He's on the track team with me. He's got something wrong with his skin. It's all white."

"Davin! That's not funny." But she laughed, and Jared thought she was pretty. She had large eyes, long eyelashes, and a nice smile, with big dimples. She was wearing bright orange shorts and a white T-shirt. "Hello, Jared," she said. "Excuse my son. He has a smart mouth."

"Do you want a Coke or something?" Davin asked Jared.

"The coach said not to drink carbonated drinks."

"Yeah, well, the coach also told us the four hundred would be good for us. So I don't believe anything *he* tells me."

From another room Jared heard a deep, round voice. "Stay off the sodas, Davin. The coach is right about that." Jared recognized the speaker. He had heard him before—sort of.

But Jared wasn't quite ready for the man who appeared at the kitchen door. He was dressed in a classy black suit, double breasted. He was something out of a men's magazine—tall and powerful, like a pro athlete. As he raised his hand to his face, Jared saw the flash of two gold rings.

He reached that same hand out to Jared. "Phil Carter," he said.

Jared shook his hand and said, "Jared Olsen." But something was running through his head. He knew that name—Phil Carter.

"Who's your father?" Mr. Carter said. Something in his voice and his presence was overpowering. It took Jared a moment to think what he had asked.

"Uh . . . Dennis Olsen. He's a—"

"*Dennis* Olsen. He went to Ogden High, didn't he?"

"Yeah."

"He and I graduated together."

"Yeah. I've heard him talk about you. You played football together, didn't you?" Jared was making the connection now. Phil Carter was a legend. Whenever Jared's dad talked about his high school days, the name always came up.

"Is that all he told you? That we *played* football?" Mr. Carter smiled, and Jared saw that taunting style of Davin's—the smile that was at least part challenge.

"Oh, no. Dad talks about you like you were the greatest athlete who ever lived."

"Don't start," Mrs. Carter said to Jared. "We hear enough about it." That warm smile of hers appeared again.

"So what's your dad doing now?" Mr. Carter asked.

"He's a chemistry professor at Weber State."

"Oh, is that right? I thought he was going to go to medical school."

"Maybe he thought about that at first. I'm not sure."

"Do you live around here?"

"Yeah. We're down off the mountain a few blocks."

Mr. Carter nodded thoughtfully.

"I remember Dad saying that you two were really close friends in high school."

"Uh-huh." Something passed through Mr. Carter's eyes, some little hesitancy. He wasn't looking at Jared straight on anymore.

Mr. Carter excused himself soon after that. He said he had to head to the airport. Davin poured some grape juice, and then he and Jared went out to the pool. As they sat down on a pair of lounge chairs Davin said, "Well, we made it, man. We survived our first four hundred." He set his drink down and reached high in the air.

Jared reached up and slapped Davin's hand, and the two of them laughed. "I just hope it gets easier," Jared said.

And Davin, still chuckling, said, "You got that right."

Jared settled back and took a long drink of grape juice. He felt pretty good now. The four hundred was going to be even worse than he had feared, but he had the feeling that he and Davin were going to get each other through it.

"It's kind of strange," Jared said. "Our dads ran together all those years ago—and were friends and everything. And now here we are, doing the same thing."

"Yeah," Davin said, but quickly. And then he looked away.

Jared wondered why, and he felt awkward after that. He ended up leaving sooner than he had thought he would.

That night, when Mr. Olsen got home, Jared was still wondering about the way Davin and Mr. Carter had reacted. He told his dad about meeting Mr. Carter.

"No kidding? Phil Carter?" Mr. Olsen said. "That's whose boy you're running with? That's amazing. I heard that a black family had built that big house up on the mountainside, but I didn't know it was Phil Carter."

"You guys were really good friends, weren't you?" Jared asked.

"Oh, yeah. Close friends. I knew Phil from kindergarten all the way through high school. I used to give him a ride home every day after football and track practice. It's unbelievable that he would show up here in Wasatch."

"Why?"

"Oh"—and suddenly there was that same strange look in Mr. Olsen's eyes—"Well . . . I just didn't know that he had done that well."

"How come you guys lost track of each other?"

"We just didn't . . . keep in touch. But listen, I'm really glad you've gotten to know his son. I hope you two will be good friends. That would really please me."

"Why?"

"Well, you know—just that Phil and I were friends. It's nice to see you two carry that on. Nowadays, that kind of friendship seems so much easier."

Jared wasn't sure what his dad meant.

"You know. Blacks and whites. That wasn't so common back in the sixties. Things were just starting to change."

"Well, Davin's a pretty good guy. But I can't really figure him out."

"Just try to get along with him, Jared. Really try. It would mean a lot to me. Did Phil . . . say anything else?"

"No."

"But he did say we were friends?"

"Yeah, he did. You *were*, weren't you?"

"Oh, yeah. Very good friends."

C h a p t e r   4

The next two weeks were tough. Some days the coach had the runners work on their starts and on speed, but most days, with the season just beginning, they worked on stamina. A couple of times Coach Heywood had the whole team run up the trail past the pond. Other days he had them do "breakdowns." That meant running five hundred meters, then four, three, on down to one hundred. All of this was done at a little less than full speed, but it was exhausting, and Jared dreaded practice every morning.

And yet, every day after practice, Jared and Davin rode their bikes up the trail. They usually stayed at the pond for a while, lying in the grass under the trees, where it was cool. But most days, once they were ready, they made an assault on the mountain. On hard workout days they didn't go far, but they pushed themselves until they had had enough. And they both liked the biking more than the running. They vowed that sooner or later they were going to make the ride all the way to the top.

Jared found that he liked Davin better all the time. One morning after their workout they were lying in the grass near the pond, talking about seventh grade and what they could expect at the junior high. "You've got to admit," Davin said, "just about all of school is stupid. We're never going to need to know any of that stuff."

Jared laughed. But then he said, "My dad says I'll understand why I need some of it once I'm grown up."

"Yeah, yeah. That's what they always say." Davin was looking up through the aspen trees, toward the sky. He was smiling. "Adults don't even believe that stuff. It just comes out of their mouths." He suddenly switched to a high-pitched voice and pumped his finger up and down like a preaching teacher. " 'How are you going to feel when someone asks you how to get to Djakarta, Indonesia—and you don't even know which direction to point? You'll have egg on your face then, won't you, young man?' "

Jared laughed. "That's one of my dad's big gripes," he said. "He's always telling me that most of the kids in the country can't find Japan on a map— stuff like that. It's like this big national shame or something."

"Yeah, well, here's how I look at it. If I want to go to Japan, I'll take a plane. I figure the pilot knows the way."

Jared laughed again.

"The coach is full of it too," Davin said, mocking Coach Heywood's gentle voice. " 'The four hundred will make a man out of you, son.' Next he's going to tell us it'll grow hair on our chests."

"The coach is okay though," Jared said.

"He's like all adults," Davin said. "He wants something from us. So he figures he's got to feed us a line—just so we'll do it."

Jared was surprised by Davin's tone of anger and resentment, with a certain edge of sadness. He didn't want to think that Davin was right, but he didn't say that.

Jared looked up through the leaves at the blue sky and he felt a numbness creeping through his tired body and even through his mind. Then a movement caught his eye, and he looked over at the water. A deer had stepped to the pond, on the opposite side. "Look," Jared whispered. "Across the pond."

Davin sat up. The doe looked around, then took another step forward and lowered her head to drink. Just then a little fawn stepped out from the trees. "Oh, wow," Davin whispered.

The two boys held silent and watched. The doe kept drinking, and the fawn stayed close to its mother, rubbing against her legs. Jared didn't move, but he glanced and saw that Davin, who was farther from the water, was slowly getting up. He took some careful, quiet steps toward the pond.

Suddenly the doe raised her head. Her big mule ears shot up. Davin froze, but the doe suddenly spun and jumped back into the trees. The fawn darted away with her. For a few seconds the deer were out of sight, and then Jared saw them bouncing up the side of the mountain.

"Oh, man, they're beautiful," Davin said. "Look how they run. It's so easy for them."

Jared heard a softness in Davin's voice that was

even more surprising than the anger he had heard just a couple of minutes before. Jared still watched the deer, but he was thinking that Davin was someone he would never really understand. Too many different things were going on inside of him.

During the week before the first meet Coach Heywood lightened the team workouts. He wanted to give the runners' legs a chance to recover. By then Jared and Davin were doing much better. They could run the four hundred at a decent pace and hold on down the final straightaway. But then, they both knew they would have to push harder in an actual race.

The track meet was with a team from North Ogden. The coach said they were one of the stronger teams in the area. Jared and Davin had been training with the four-by-one-hundred relay team, and both had worked on the long jump. But Jared hardly thought about those events. All his concentration—and nervousness—was directed toward the four hundred.

The meet was held on the Wasatch track on a Saturday morning. Jared played the whole thing down to his family. "It's just a warm-up—not a real meet," he told them. "In fact, none of these meets really counts for anything—except for the last one, where we try to qualify for the state championships."

His mom and Lori took him seriously, but both his dad and Kent showed up anyway.

Just before the first event Coach Heywood explained the schedule. The four-by-one-hundred was right before the four hundred. Jared felt his stomach grab at the thought. But the coach said, "Remember, we have girls' and boys' events in all the age categories. You'll have plenty of time to recover. Really, running the relay first is a good way to warm up."

Jared wasn't so sure. And Davin complained all through the first three events, until the time came for the relay.

Jared ran the first leg of the relay, and he got his usual good start. But then the North Ogden runner caught him, and things went downhill from there. The Wasatch team had better handoffs than North Ogden, but they still lost by twenty meters.

In one sense, the coach was right. The one hundred hadn't taken much out of Jared. But now, after being beaten so badly, his confidence had taken another dive. The Wasatch kids were losing most of the races, and that didn't help either.

Jared and Davin walked onto the track as soon as the girls in the same age category finished their race. "I want to get this over with," Davin said, and Jared nodded. He was feeling sick at his stomach.

"Give it all you've got, Jared!" Mr. Olsen yelled from the bleachers. Jared saw Kent and his dad sitting side by side. Never before had it struck him quite how much alike they were. They were not as long legged as Jared, but they were well proportioned and athletic; both had the same dark hair and even the same high forehead. Jared was more like his mother, light-haired and skinny. And his mom was a klutz at anything athletic.

Jared saw Kent climb down from the bleachers

and walk to the edge of the track. "Jared," he said, "don't get suckered into running too hard at first. Just cruise the first turn and stay close. You'll need something left at the end."

Kent sounded nervous, and that only made things worse. Jared nodded, but he didn't say anything. He walked over and got his starting blocks set, and then he looked at Davin. "How are you feeling?" he asked.

"Hey, I'm fine," Davin said. "I'll run the stupid race, but I'm not going to kill myself."

And yet, Jared could see that Davin was scared. He had never realized that black skin could turn pale—sort of gray—as Davin's was now.

He was thinking exactly that when Davin said, "Whoa, Jared, you look white as a sheet."

"Do I? So do you," Jared said. "I just noticed that."

"Hey, bro, don't tell *me* that," Davin said. "I ain't never going to be *no shade* of white."

Jared smiled, but he was embarrassed. "I'm sorry. I didn't mean—"

Davin's eyes flashed. "Hey, you don't have to *apologize*," he said.

Jared didn't know what to make of this brief exchange. In some ways he felt annoyed. But the starter was calling the runners to their blocks, and he had to focus on that now. Jared heard his dad yell, "Okay, Jared, go after those guys."

In response, it seemed, Mr. Carter's deep voice resounded from the side of the track. "Smoke these guys, Davin." He must have just arrived. Jared hadn't seen him earlier.

Jared walked to his blocks. He was in the second lane, and the start was staggered. No one was running in lane one, so he would be able to see the other four runners. Two North Ogden runners were in lanes three and four, then Davin, and then one more from North Ogden. The black kid in lane three was supposed to be the fastest, from what Jared had heard.

Jared took his time getting into his blocks. He knew the routine now. He kicked his legs, stretched them, settled in slowly, and then looked down the track, down the white lines that stretched ahead and then curved off to the left. He felt tight in his chest, out of breath before he started.

"*Seeehhhhhhhhht.*"

Jared pushed his legs up under him, lifting his rear end high in the air. His breath caught, and he felt ready to explode. He heard his own voice, inside his head, screaming, "*Let's go. Let's go. Let's go.*"

The gun fired and Jared drove forward, hard—and way too fast. He made up some of the stagger on the guy in lane three—and he knew he had to ease off.

And so he let himself coast around the turn, giving back the couple of steps he had gained. The guy in lane four was staying about even with the stagger too, but Davin was dropping back. So was the guy out in lane six.

All down the backstretch Jared stayed close, and a timer in his head said that he was going too fast. Kent had said not to get suckered. Maybe he had done that already.

At the start of the second turn the pain came on suddenly, jabbing through his thighs and then his calves. Something also caught inside, jerking down on his collarbone. But he told himself not to give in to the pain. He had to keep driving, keep loose, keep his arms pumping.

Outside his head somewhere, across the track, he could hear his teammates shouting, as though from another world. He saw the white lines slip by his sides. He saw a blur of black track and some gray-blue sky rushing by. Inside he heard only the soft sound of his spikes. But all that was vague and unreal. Reality was the pain in his chest and legs, the sickness.

Halfway through the turn he knew for sure that he had started too fast. His thighs suddenly locked, and he felt his rhythm break. He tried to drive his knees but couldn't. His stride was shortening with every step.

The two guys to his right were leaving him behind. He was more or less even with Davin, and the guy in lane six was slipping back. But Jared didn't care. All he wanted to do was end the pain. *Hang on,* he kept telling himself. *Finish. Somehow. Finish.*

He heard his dad and Kent yelling to him from outside his tunnel of numbness. But it didn't matter. Nothing mattered but getting to the finish line.

And then he gave way to the pain. He staggered and slowed almost to a walk as he crossed the finish line. He walked on for five or six steps, and sank to his knees on the track. Then he bent forward, with his arms on the track, supporting his head. All he wanted was for the world to leave him alone. But some guy had him by the shoulder. "You were third," he said.

Jared didn't care. "Don't," he said, but he wasn't even sure what he meant.

And then his dad was there. "Good race, son," he said.

Kent's voice was there too. "Fun race, huh?" He laughed. "Feel like you're going to lose your breakfast?"

Jared almost did. But he swallowed and took a long breath, and the peak of the nausea passed. In another few seconds he managed to look up at his dad and brother.

Coach Heywood came over and knelt down by him. He wrapped an arm around his shoulder. "You okay?"

Jared didn't respond.

"Hey, that wasn't bad for a first time. The two boys who beat you were older, and they're some of the better runners around here. You take two seconds off that time, maybe three, and you'll be competitive."

Jared knew he couldn't do it. He told himself he would never push any harder than he just had.

His dad was laughing. "He's got enough speed," he told the coach. "He just has to build his stamina for the old gut-check time."

Jared wasn't really listening. He was drawing in air. But then he heard Mr. Carter's voice. "I can't believe you let those kids outrun you down the straightaway. Don't you have one lick of pride? You didn't even try."

Jared remembered that he had beaten Davin. He was surprised. But it still wasn't important to him.

"I *did* try," he heard Davin say softly.

Jared saw that Davin was bending over, grasping his knees, breathing hard. His red tank top was soaked with sweat.

"Yeah, you tried about as hard as you *usually* try," his dad said. "Just hard enough to get by."

Mr. Olsen was looking at Mr. Carter. Jared saw the impulse in his dad's face to say something, but Mr. Olsen held back.

"Come on, son, you need to keep moving," he said. "Walk a little and then jog a lap. You need to cool down before you stiffen up. You still have to long jump, don't you?"

The thought was depressing. Jared didn't think he could jump far enough to make the pit. But slowly he was feeling better, and after he walked and then jogged a little, long jumping didn't sound impossible. At least the worst was over.

Will Belliston and some of the older runners talked to him too, said he had run a good race for a first try. "You could be really good at that distance," Will told him.

"I'm not sure I want to be," he said. "It hurts too much."

"Yeah. But I think you've got the guts to get in shape for it. Carter probably doesn't."

"I think he does," Jared said.

"Maybe. But I doubt it."

Jared didn't ask why Will felt that way. He let the subject go. But he wondered what Will was actually thinking.

Jared walked over to the long jump pit. As it turned out, he was able to jump about as well as usual, but he wasn't in the same league with the better long jumpers. He made up his mind not to enter the bigger meets. He would only embarrass himself.

When the meet was over, the coach had a few things to say about working harder in the coming weeks if the runners wanted to be competitive. All Jared could think was that he wished track season were over.

When the coach was finished, Davin and Jared walked away together. Jared noticed that his dad, Kent, and Mr. Carter were standing near the end of the bleachers, talking. Mr. Carter was wearing a dress shirt and tie, and Jared figured he was on his way to some business meeting.

When the boys approached, Mr. Olsen said, "Hey, this is great to have an Olsen and a Carter running together again." He looked at Davin. "Your dad and I have some great memories." Then he laughed. "Of course, anytime I ran against your dad, the only thing I got to look at was his back."

Jared watched Mr. Carter. He didn't smile, didn't even acknowledge the comment. Jared suspected, for one thing, that he was still upset about Davin's poor showing. By now Jared had found out that Davin had finished fourth, but the kid in the outside lane had stopped when he was coming down the stretch. Davin had run out of gas and lost to Jared by three or four steps.

"I'll tell you," Mr. Olsen said, "your dad was a superstar in football too. With his size and speed, he used to *demolish* those high school linebackers—just run right over the top of them. He was a starter when he was a sophomore. I didn't get to start until I was a senior."

"Well, it was nice to see you, Dennis," Mr. Carter said formally, and he turned to walk away.

"Let's get together sometime," Mr. Olsen said.

Mr. Carter nodded, but he didn't say anything.

Mr. Olsen hurried to catch up and then walked alongside him. "My son tells me you've had a lot of success," he said.

"I've done pretty well," Mr. Carter said. "Better than anyone around here ever expected, I'm sure."

"What exactly did you—"

But Mr. Carter had reached the gate, and he turned to his left, toward his parked Mercedes. "Well, anyway, nice to see you again," he said, and walked away.

"Yeah. I'm sure I'll be seeing you," Mr. Olsen said. But Mr. Carter didn't look back.

Chapter 5

Mr. Olsen didn't say much on the way home. But Kent had lots of advice. All Jared had to do was knock a second off his time each week, and he would soon be beating guys like the ones who had beaten him today. Jared thought, Yeah, and maybe those guys will knock a second off each week too; but he didn't say it.

When he got home he went to his room and lay down. His legs were killing him, but even more, he was feeling sick again. The air-conditioning felt good. He thought he might stay right on that bed the rest of the day.

Jared hadn't been in his room long before his mom came in and sat down on the bed. "Are you really wiped out, honey?" she said. She ran the cool palm of her hand across his forehead.

But this wasn't really like Mom. Jared smiled. "What's this," he asked, "your tender mother act?"

She leaned back and laughed, her face coloring. "You know me too well, kiddo. I always wanted to be one of those homey little mothers with flour all over my apron and cookies in the oven. But it just isn't in me, is it?" She ran her fingers through her short hair, pushing some loose strands behind her ears. "When did you become such a smart aleck anyway?"

"I don't know. Maybe I picked it up somewhere around here."

"Well, anyway, are you okay?"

"Yeah."

"Did you get enough rah-rah speeches from your dad and brother to last you for a while?"

"Yeah. Mostly from Kent."

"Was the race really awful?"

"I thought I was going to *die*—that's all."

She grimaced, and he could see how much it really did hurt her. "Oh, honey, won't the coach let you run something else?"

"I'm not fast enough for the sprints. And I don't want to run anything longer."

She nodded, but she still looked concerned.

"It's okay," Jared said. "I'll get through it. But I'm never going to be as fast as Kent."

"Jared, so what? Someday when you're both shuffling papers in some office, or doctoring, or whatever—who's going to ask you how fast you could run when you were a kid?"

Jared wished he could think of it that way. But he thought of his dad and Mr. Carter. It still mattered to them how fast they had run when they were kids.

The next week at practice, Davin and Jared trained harder. "I don't care if I run the race faster," Jared told Davin between hard breaths. "I just want to get around the track without feeling like my legs are turning to stone."

"Yeah, well, I wish it was that easy for me," Davin said. He and Jared had just finished running three hundred meters at "three-quarter speed," as the coach called it. In another couple of minutes they would have to do a four hundred at the same pace.

They were getting close to the end of a double breakdown. They had run five hundred, four hundred, down to one hundred meters, and now they were working their way back up to five.

"What do you mean?" Jared asked.

"My dad says I've got to do better this week. He says I was dogging it last time."

"You weren't, though, were you?"

"Sure I was. Do you think a white guy like you could beat me if I was really trying?" Jared laughed, and yet, he wasn't sure; maybe Davin meant it.

The boys made it through the double breakdown, encouraging each other all the way. And when practice was over they rode their bikes to the pond. They rested longer than usual, and once their legs recovered they made a pretty good push at the mountain.

The first part of the trail was not bad, steep in only a few places and fairly steady. But after about half a mile the trail made a switchback and turned severely uphill. They had to gear down and work from that point on.

Jared took the lead. He was still in better shape for biking than Davin. He pushed up the big climb that angled across the front of the mountain. The view was fantastic, but he only took a quick glance a couple of times. Right now it was just pump, pump, pump and keep his eyes on the rocky trail.

Jared wanted to make it to the second switchback. He thought that was about halfway to the top. The boys had actually gone beyond that turn a couple of times—but not on days when they had worked so hard on the track.

They were maybe three-fourths of the way up the incline when Davin said, "Hey, man, I can't make it today. Aren't you dying?"

Jared was actually relieved. He stopped and put a foot down. Then, after catching his breath a little, he got off his bike and set it down. Davin had already done the same thing. The two of them sat on the edge of the trail in the dry grass. The mountainside was dotted with sagebrush and rabbitbrush, but there were no trees. The sun was hot.

"We're stupid," Davin said between breaths. He pulled up the front of his shirt and tried to wipe the sweat from his face, but the tank top was soaked through already. "Nobody's even making us do this."

Jared took a look at the view. Beneath them was his neighborhood, and out beyond was the Uinta Valley near the mouth of Weber Canyon. In the distance was the Great Salt Lake, gray and shading to green. Back toward Ogden, to the north, there was an amber haze of pollution hanging in the valley. But the Uinta Valley, where the wind always blew, was clear.

Jared pulled his old baseball cap off and fanned his face. "Man, it's hot," he said.

Davin was wiping sweat from his face with the palm of his hand. He rubbed it on his shorts. "We ought to be sitting by my pool with my CD player cranked."

"That's exactly right. Why do we do this?"

Davin slid down farther off the trail, lay back, and put his hands behind his head. "I don't know," he said. "I really don't."

Jared also lay back. He watched a couple of puffy summer clouds that were floating overhead. "Do you think it really helps us?"

"It helps us with our wind, I guess."

"How much does your dad say you have to improve this time?"

"I don't know. He doesn't give me a time. He just tells me I've got to do a lot better. What he means, really, is that I have to beat *you*."

Jared sat up and looked at Davin. "Really?"

"Of course." Davin wouldn't look at Jared.

"Why?"

Davin laughed. "Because you're white, for one thing."

Jared couldn't think what to say. He stared at Davin. "Are you serious?"

"It's not just you. After we got home last week my dad kept saying, 'I can't believe you let those white boys beat you.' " Davin didn't bother to imitate his dad's voice. He wasn't playing now.

Jared looked back at the valley. He had never suspected anything like this. He hardly knew what to say. "Davin, my parents have been teaching me my whole life that everybody's the same—no matter what color they are."

"Yeah, *right*."

Jared was more surprised than ever. "Don't you believe that?"

"That color shouldn't matter?"

"Yeah."

"Oh, sure. I believe it. But I don't think your parents do. Not really. Neither do you."

"What are you talking about?"

"Look, Jared, let's just forget it."

"Don't you want to keep biking together and—"

"Hey, sure. It doesn't matter. All I'm saying is that you may think you don't care about color, but you do. *Everyone* does. That's just the way it is. But it's not worth talking about."

Davin got up and walked back to his bike. He lifted his duffel bag off the back and pulled out a white T-shirt. He used it to wipe the sweat from his face and neck, and then his arms.

Jared was trying to think what to say. He didn't want to let the subject drop. Finally he said, "Then how come you don't just hang around with black guys?"

"Do you see a lot of choices around here? There wasn't a black guy in our whole school. And there won't be many at the junior high. J. C. is the only one on the track team, and he's a jerk."

"But is that what you'd do if you could—have only black friends?"

"I don't know, Jared." For the first time Davin

sounded irritated. "I just find a way to get by." He held the T-shirt with both hands and wiped it over his face again.

"Davin, I don't even know what you're talking about."

"I know you don't. That's why it's not worth getting into. Come on. Let's ride back down."

"No. Tell me. If I'm against blacks, how come we're up here together?"

"I didn't say you were *against* blacks."

"What are you saying then?"

Davin dropped the T-shirt back into the duffel bag. He looked down at Jared. "I don't fit in anywhere, Jared. And I never will. At school I'm the only black guy, and I *never* forget that—not for one second of the day."

"Hey, I know I'm white all the time. What difference does that make?"

"Oh, man. Think about it. How would you feel at a school where everyone was black, and you were the only white kid?"

Jared sensed that he would be uncomfortable, but he didn't like the idea. "That wouldn't mean that anyone was against me. It would just be sort of . . ." But Jared didn't know what it would be. Why *would* he feel strange?

"Jared, you don't know because you haven't done it. Kids say things. They . . ." But Davin couldn't seem to come up with the words to explain what he meant.

"Do they call you names or something?"

"No. Well, yeah. A couple of times. But those are

the guys who really are *against* blacks. But that's not what I'm talking about. It's mostly just everyone being sort of . . . careful . . . around me. They don't treat me the same way they do white kids."

"I've never noticed that."

"Yeah, right. What about the other day when you said I looked white—and then you thought you had to tell me you were sorry."

Jared stood up and faced Davin. "I didn't at first. But you acted like I'd said the wrong thing—so I thought maybe I had."

"I was just joking with you."

"You say stuff like that all the time, Davin. I can't tell when you're joking. I never know what I can say around you."

"That's because you think you have to be *careful*. That's the whole point. You know you're not like that when you're around Nick." Davin turned away from Jared, bent down, and picked up a rock. He gave it a quick flick and then watched it arc into the valley below.

Jared was thinking. He wanted to be honest. "I don't think I'm different around you from the way I am with any of my other friends."

Davin laughed. "I know you *think* that, Jared."

Jared was frustrated by now, and a little angry. "Look, I just thought we were friends."

Davin laughed in that offhand "I know more than you do" style of his that was so maddening.

"Aren't we friends?" Jared asked.

"Sure," he said. "We're *best buddies*—until Nick, your white friend, gets back."

Jared didn't know what to say. Maybe he was closer friends with Nick. Maybe he always would be. But he didn't think it had anything to do with race. He reached down and picked up his bike. Maybe he wouldn't hang around with Davin anymore. "I think you're the one who's prejudiced, Davin. You blame it on your dad, but I think you don't like whites either."

Davin bent down and grabbed his duffel bag, then picked up his bike and slid the bag under the bungee cord. When he turned the bike around, Jared was still facing him.

"You're the one who brings up race all the time."

"I'm just trying to get you to . . ." Davin stopped and shook his head. "Look, forget it."

"No. Say what you were going to say."

Davin was holding on to the handlebars on his bike. He looked down at the ground. "Can't you see what it's like, Jared? I get tired of everybody *pretending*. It's like everyone wants me to think they don't notice I'm black. I just want to say, 'Hey, it's okay. You can mention it.' "

"Yeah, but you don't just mention it. You put people down."

"No, I don't. It's just . . . stuff I say. We did that all the time up in Portland."

"It seems like more than just joking around."

Davin took a long breath and then let it out, slowly. "Look, Jared, there's one thing I already know. I'm never going to have a friend in this town. Not really. Not a close friend."

"You won't if you make up your mind ahead of time. Do you even *want* to have friends?"

"Yeah, Jared. I do," Davin said. "But I know how things are."

"Davin, our dads were friends way back in the sixties. And that didn't happen much back then. I don't see why—"

"Is that what you really think?" Davin smiled, and that superior tone of his had returned.

"What?"

"Do you really think they were good friends?"

"Don't you?"

"Hey, I *know* they weren't. My dad *hates* your dad."

"What?" Jared asked. And yet, he wasn't as surprised as he wanted to be.

"You heard me. That's one of the reasons I have to beat you."

Jared was out of responses. He wanted to talk this all out, but he didn't know what to say.

Davin pushed his bike past Jared, then got on and let it coast down the trail. He had to weave in and out of the rocks.

Jared followed and tried to think. But he felt lost. Things he had always thought he had known, understood, suddenly weren't making sense.

And yet, strangely, nothing changed with Davin after that. The routine the rest of the week was exactly the same. Each morning the boys trained together, and they talked and joked. After the workout they took their ride. In fact, the next day, when the coach had them do mostly speed work and their legs were fresh, they pushed well past the halfway point, farther than ever before.

But it was all so awkward for Jared. How could

Davin say all those things and then just go back to business as usual? And yet, as Jared thought back on the conversation, he remembered Davin's sadness more than his biting words. And he remembered Davin saying, yes, that he would like to have a friend.

Chapter 6

The next track meet involved several teams from northern Utah. It was held on a high school track in Clearfield, a town not far from Wasatch. The coach asked both Mr. Olsen and Mr. Carter if they would drive some of the runners to the meet.

Jared thought Davin might stay away from him that morning, since his dad would be there. But Davin came right over while Jared was stretching.

"Do you want to jog a couple of laps to warm up?" Jared asked.

"Hey, I never *want* to jog a couple of laps. But I guess I will. At least one."

The two jogged in their athletic shoes, not their spikes. Jared noticed that Davin had a new pair. "Those are nice shoes," he told Davin.

"Yeah, they're cross-trainers." He skipped and raised one foot so Jared could get a better look.

"My parents won't get me shoes like that. They say I wear them out too fast, and they cost too much."

"Yeah, well, my dad will spend money on anything he thinks will get me more interested in sports. Besides, I think he likes to go into a store and say, 'We want the best shoe you've got,' and then watch these white salesmen run around to wait on him."

Jared laughed a little, because Davin was laughing. Regardless of their talk on the mountain, he still didn't want to say the wrong thing. He didn't want to seem too "careful" either.

"I wish the four hundred was over with," Jared said, just to get them back to common ground.

"Me too," Davin said. "It's good I only have to beat you—and not some really fast guys."

Jared didn't say anything, but just chuckled.

"You don't think you can beat *me* again, do you?" Davin asked.

For some reason, he was needling, almost as though he wanted Jared to take him on. Jared was tempted to say, "I'm faster than you are. I proved that last race." Instead, he said, "I don't care if I beat *anybody*. I just want to survive."

"Yeah, you say that. But I've got a feeling you're going to go for it today. You *know* you want to show me what you can do."

Actually, Jared had been thinking mostly about the pain he had felt the week before. And yet, Davin's attitude was annoying. Although he hadn't actually said anything about color this time, Jared still felt uncomfortable.

Davin only jogged one lap, but Jared went on for two. Then he came back and did some more stretching exercises and practiced some starts. During the early events he tried to keep moving to stay loose. It was a warm morning, which he liked. He had let his legs rest a good deal the last two days, and he really did feel strong.

Jared also felt better about the way he ran in the relay this time. He got a good start, and his legs felt full of snap. Eventually the faster guys went by him, but he stayed closer. The Wasatch runners finished fourth out of five teams, but at least they beat someone. The success, no matter how small, relaxed Jared a little and gave him some confidence.

By the time the announcer called his race, however, the nervousness was back. Kent hadn't come this morning—which was good—but Jared knew his dad would hope for a faster time than Jared had run the week before.

Davin was in lane two and Jared was in lane four. A guy from Clearfield was between them. He was no taller than Jared, but he looked a lot older. He wasn't built like a runner, not long-legged and sleek, but he looked strong. Jared had heard that he was the guy to beat. A couple of kids from Ogden, one from Sunset, and a runner from Roy filled out the outer lanes. A really short kid from Logan was in lane one.

With the staggered start Jared knew he wouldn't see Davin during the early part of the race. He told himself to run his race and not think about Davin, but he knew at the same time that he *did* want to beat him.

As Jared and Davin set their blocks, Mr. Carter walked down to the edge of the track. "All right, son," he said, "let's see you do something today."

It sounded more like a warning than encouragement. Davin shrugged, as if to say, "Don't expect too much." Jared thought he looked scared, and felt sorry for him. But he told himself that he hadn't created the situation, and there was nothing he could do about it. He took a couple more practice starts and then walked to his blocks and waited.

The muscles in his legs were twitching. And once the starter called him to the blocks, and he got set, his whole body felt wound like a spring.

When the gun fired, Jared came out of the blocks digging like a sprinter. He made up the stagger on the guy in lane five, and the runners in the inner lanes were nowhere in sight—not even the guy in lane three, who was supposed to be so fast.

Hold back. Hold back, he kept telling himself, but his legs wanted to go. He felt strong and light and fast. He could hear the runner in the third lane, knew he was not far back, but he didn't seem to be gaining.

Jared kept cruising, not pushing, but feeling good down the backstretch. There were fewer people at this meet, and on the back side of the track he could hardly hear anyone cheering. He could hear the gentle rush of the light wind past his ears, and he knew he would have a slight breeze with him for the kick down the stretch.

For now he was just out there, moving well, and he liked the sensation. The pain was still waiting for him, but he knew already that it wouldn't be as bad today. The soft *thump, thump* of the track under his spikes seemed to spring him forward with every stride. He had passed the guy in lane five and moved

60

up on the runners in the outer lanes. He knew he could get them in the turn.

As Jared started into the curve he finally felt the Clearfield guy coming up on him. He pushed himself a little harder, and for the first time felt the strain. But it wasn't bad. He was starting to hurt, his chest beginning to burn, but he was still lifting his knees, and his thighs weren't tightening—not yet.

Coming out of the turn, the Clearfield runner moved alongside him, and now it was just a straightaway to see who had the most left. Jared remembered what the coach had told him.

Run relaxed. Don't tighten your hands. Swing your arms.

But "the wall" was waiting for him. It had only held off longer today. Without warning, Jared felt his stride break, felt his legs tighten. His feet began to hit the track harder, heavier. He wasn't dying—not the way he had before—but he was losing power. And the Clearfield guy was moving ahead. Jared fought to stay with him, but the pain was really setting in now, and his legs kept slowing.

And then he realized that Davin was coming up on him too. Jared only sensed his advance at first, but then he took a quick glance. Davin was a step back and pushing, really trying this time. But he was losing speed too.

Down the stretch they went. All the runners in the outside lanes had dropped back and the Clearfield guy was moving well ahead. Jared's race was now with Davin.

Jared kept driving his arms, lifting his knees. His legs were giving out, but he wanted to hang on, wanted to beat Davin. He heard his dad yelling at him, his voice like words in his own head—there but not there. "Hang on, Jared. Hang on," he was shouting from the bleachers.

And then Mr. Carter's big voice came booming in, louder. "Davin, *push! Get him! Get him!*"

Jared gave one last lunge and threw himself across the line. He staggered ahead a few steps and then bent over. He was tired, but to his own surprise, he wasn't hurting as badly as he had the time before. He was gasping for air, but he wasn't sick.

One of the finish judges, a high school boy, came up to him and got his name. "I think you were second," he said. "But it was really close. I've got to see what the other judges say."

Jared stood up straight and took deep breaths. He saw Mr. Carter standing in front of Davin. He wasn't speaking loudly, the way he had the time before, but he seemed to be giving Davin a pretty good chewing out again.

Coach Heywood came out on the track and said, "Davin, Jared, good work. You both improved a lot over last week. I told you those breakdowns would pay off." He laughed.

"Jared!" Jared looked over and saw his dad, who had come down to the edge of the track. "Good job!" he said.

Jared walked over to him.

"Second place. That's great!"

"That guy said it was really close. I might have gotten third. They haven't decided yet."

His dad looked surprised. "Oh, no. You were second. It wasn't *that* close."

Jared nodded. He was pleased—but not quite as much as he had expected to be. He wondered about Davin. His dad was probably really angry.

"I timed your run. You improved by almost two seconds. Can you believe that? The coach said that you needed to pick up two or three seconds to be competitive. But I never thought you'd knock off that much in a week."

Jared nodded. He was still trying to get his breath.

"It felt better too, didn't it?" his father said.

"Yeah. Quite a bit."

"By the end of the season, if you keep working hard, you'll be tough to beat. I can't remember whether Kent ever ran the four hundred at your age, but I doubt he could have done any better."

Dad was happy. He was probably beginning to think that his second son was also going to be a track star. Jared liked that. He really did. But he had to wonder how fast he would have to run in the next meet to keep his dad this happy.

"Okay," a judge called out, "for second and third, it was pretty much a dead heat. But we called it Carter second, Olsen third."

"What?" Mr. Olsen whispered to Jared. "That can't be right."

"I guess he got me," Jared said to his dad. But he didn't believe it. He had been sure at the time that he had held Davin off at the finish.

"No way, Jared." Mr. Olsen sounded upset, but then he added, quickly, "But don't say anything to Davin. Just be a good sport about it. These things can happen with amateur judges. It's just good it was

Davin, and not a guy from another team."

"Yeah," Jared said. And he tried to think that way. But he didn't like it. He looked across the track and saw that Mr. Carter was giving Davin a pat on the back—accepting the judges' decision. That bothered Jared even more.

He walked back to the infield and put his warm-ups on. He knew he needed to do some cool-down jogging. He tried to tell himself that he didn't care about the judges' decision, but the anger was growing in him.

When he saw Davin coming he sat down quickly and began to change his shoes. He didn't want to talk right now.

But Davin stopped in front of him. "Why did they do that?" he asked.

"Do what?" Jared didn't look up.

"Why did they give me second?"

"I guess you beat me."

"You *know* I didn't."

Jared didn't answer. He was tying a shoelace, and he kept his head down.

"What are they trying to do?"

Davin sounded angry, which Jared didn't understand at all. He finally looked up. "It's not that important," he said.

"What are you talking about, Jared? Why don't you go say something to the judges?"

"What for? It doesn't matter to me. We finished right together."

Davin was staring at Jared. "I can't believe you," he finally said. "And I can't believe all those white judges."

"Davin, what are you talking about? They gave it to *you*, not to *me*."

"That's right. They *gave* it to me."

Now Jared had heard everything. Davin was nuts! But Jared didn't say that. He got to his feet. "I don't know what happened, Davin," he said. "Did your dad think you won?"

"No—not at first. But he was more than happy not to believe his own eyes. What did your dad say?"

Jared shrugged. "I don't know. I guess he thought . . . it was really close."

Davin laughed. "Jared, you make me sick sometimes," he said, and walked away.

Jared shook his head. He just didn't know how to deal with Davin. But Jared knew he had beaten him, and he wished now that he had had the guts to say so.

When the meet was over, Jared and his dad walked toward the stadium gate together. Near the gate Phil Carter and Davin were waiting for some of the kids who were riding with them. Jared's dad walked over to Phil and shook his hand. And then he congratulated Davin. "Well, Phil, the boys looked better today, didn't they?" he said.

Mr. Carter had on an expensive pair of dress slacks and a yellow knit shirt. "Yes, they did very well," he said, but he sounded reserved.

Mr. Olsen chuckled to himself. "Do you think they could outrun us in a two-man relay?"

"I think maybe *I* could beat them," said Davin's dad. "But you're packing a little more weight than you used to." He smiled, as though he had intended only a friendly little jab, but the words had sounded more like a challenge. Jared heard the same tone he had heard from Davin lots of times.

"Boy, that's for sure," Mr. Olsen said. "I just don't get time to work out anymore. I really need to." He patted his middle, which did bulge a little.

"I *make* time," Mr. Carter said.

"I ought to."

"Hey, I'd think a schoolteacher would have more time than I do. And you've got the gym and track right there on campus."

Jared could tell that his dad was uncomfortable. And Jared was feeling the same way. He kept glancing over at Davin, but Davin wouldn't look back at him.

Mr. Olsen let the subject go. He said, "Phil, we really ought to get together. I'd like to have our wives get to know each other. Any chance you could come over tonight—or maybe tomorrow afternoon? We could barbecue some steaks or something."

"I'm afraid I'm tied up this weekend," Mr. Carter said. "I'm leaving town again, and I have some things I have to take care of before I go." Then he turned to Davin and said, "Come on, son. We need to get going."

"Will you be back next weekend?"

"Uh . . . maybe." He wouldn't look at Mr. Olsen now.

"How about next Saturday then?"

"I kind of doubt it, Dennis. This is a busy time for me."

"Well, okay. But sometime we've got to do that."

"Yeah. Maybe sometime," Mr. Carter said as he walked away.

Davin turned to leave with him, but Jared said, "I'll see you tomorrow."

"Yeah," Davin said, distantly, and he walked away with his father.

C h a p t e r 7

Monday morning at track practice Coach Heywood didn't push the team too hard. He said he knew the runners were still sore from the meet on Saturday. "But starting tomorrow," he told them, "come ready to work. We have no meet this week, so we have some time to go hard and get everyone in better shape."

Jared had half expected Davin to avoid him, but Davin looked toward Jared with that solid, confident expression of his, and he said, "Sounds like a fun week." The old sarcasm was there, and his eyes slid past Jared's, never quite making contact.

But Davin didn't drag himself through the training runs that day. And after, on their bike ride, he led out, and he kept pounding away at the mountain, well past their previous high point.

When he finally stopped, Jared said, "What got into you today?" He took a couple of quick, deep breaths. "I thought you were never going to stop."

Davin still had one leg over his bike. He was leaning over the handlebars, breathing hard. "Did I really push you?" he said between breaths. "Could you have gone farther?"

"Not much. I almost yelled for you to stop." Jared put down his bike and sat down in the grass below the trail.

"Why didn't you?"

"I didn't want to be the first one to give up." He ran his hand over his wet crew cut, setting off a little spray of sweat.

"I wish I'd kept going a little longer," Davin said. "Maybe you would have quit."

"No way," Jared said, and he grinned.

Davin seemed to like that. He laughed and said, "We'll see about that. I'm going to get you one of these days." Davin put his bike down and then sprawled on the ground. He lay in the grass for a couple of minutes, until his breathing slowed. Then, without looking at Jared, he said, "I'm going to beat you in the next four hundred too."

Jared remembered the touchy moment at the track meet. He wasn't sure what he should say. He hesitated and then said, "You did last time. So I guess you will again."

But Davin stiffened, and when he spoke, his voice had changed. The taunting tone was back. "So do you still think our dads are good friends?"

"What do you mean?"

"Couldn't you see what was going on the other day—after the track meet?"

"Your dad was just kidding around, wasn't he?"

"Don't give me that." Davin sat up and looked at

Jared. "All that stuff about being a lot busier than your dad—and your dad being fat—what do you think that was? I don't see why your dad just smiles and takes all that stuff."

Jared had already thought about that. "I think my dad does want to be friends—so he didn't make a big deal out of it."

"Yeah, well, if he thinks we're coming over for dinner, he better think again. That would only happen if Dad had you guys over to *our* house—and then he'd only do it to show off."

"What do you mean?"

Davin looked out across the valley. "We don't live in a house, Jared. You saw it. It's a showplace. Dad takes people through it on *tours*. It's his way of proving that he's *important*." Davin deepened his voice. "'Oh, did I show you my hot tub? It's the biggest in the universe.'"

Jared couldn't help laughing. But he said, "Hey, he's done well. So what if he shows off a little?"

"Jared, why do you always do that?"

"Do what?"

"Try to explain everything away. Pretend that . . . things aren't the way they are."

"I'm not. I'm just saying—"

"My dad moved out here *because* this is an all-white neighborhood, and he built the biggest house in the whole area. It's his way of saying, 'Look at me, white boys. I'm one step above you.' And there are some people around Wasatch who don't like it one bit either."

Jared was suddenly uncomfortable again. "Maybe

so, Davin. I don't know," he said. "But lots of poor kids do that. My dad was poor growing up too, and I'm sure he was also trying to prove something by moving out here."

"That's just it, Jared. It doesn't prove anything. It doesn't work."

Jared didn't know what Davin meant. He decided he better just let the subject drop before the two of them got into another argument.

But Davin said, "Why do you think those white judges put me ahead of you the other day?"

Jared blew out his breath. "I don't know, Davin. But if they were prejudiced they would have given it to *me*. That's the only thing that makes sense."

Davin laughed. "Maybe that's how it used to be— like down in the South, or something. But now it's just the opposite. I can just hear all those white guys saying, 'If we say the white kid won, someone might say we're prejudiced. So we'll prove what good, fair white folks we are. We'll *give it* to the black boy.'"

"Come on, Davin. That wouldn't happen."

"How do you know, Jared? Whites figure that's the only thing blacks can do—run fast. And play basketball. So let them have that much."

"Oh, give me a break, Davin. You're just looking for something to be mad about." Jared had reacted without thinking, and already he was wishing he could take the words back. But he was growing tired of Davin's dragging race into everything.

But Davin seemed to like the challenge. He laughed and pointed a finger right at Jared's nose. "Okay, then, you tell me why they called it the way they did.

Everyone in the whole place knew you beat me."

"I don't know, Davin. Maybe they just blew it—just made a mistake."

"Why didn't anyone protest? Why didn't your dad? Why didn't *you*?"

"What good would that do?"

"Come on. Think about it, Jared. If you had beaten some white kid and the judges had called it the other way, you and your dad both would have been over there complaining."

Jared wasn't sure. Maybe that was true. It was his dad who had told him to be a "good sport." Maybe that was because he didn't want to take on Mr. Carter. But Jared was tired of trying to think about all this stuff. He leaned over and cupped his forehead with his hand. "I don't know, Davin. I don't know what I would have done."

"But you do admit you beat me?"

"Yeah. I beat you." Jared hesitated, and then he added, "Not by much. But I think I beat you."

Davin looked pleased. "Well, you're not going to beat me next time, white boy," he said.

Jared didn't answer. A kind of anger was swelling in him that said, We'll see about that. And yet, another side of him was saying, If it means that much to him, let him have it.

"Didn't you hear me? I told you I'm going to beat you next time. Don't you have anything to say about that?"

"No. I'll let you talk. And I'll run."

It was a good comeback, and Jared expected an angry reaction. But what he got was a big smile. "All right. You're on. We're going to find out who the *man* is." Davin looked strangely satisfied with the idea.

"I don't get you, Davin," Jared said. "I thought you didn't care about running. I thought you were only trying to keep your dad happy."

Davin's eyes dropped. After a few seconds he looked up and shrugged. "Jared, I don't know why I do most of the things I do. Do you ever feel that way?"

Jared thought about that for a time, then said, "Yeah, I guess so." It was a strange moment. Jared knew he was tired of all this thinking, of all of the unnecessary challenges. But he also knew he was, in some sense, saying thank you to Davin.

Davin seemed to know it too. They said nothing more, but as his annoyance passed, Jared liked the way he felt. He was confused, but he had the idea that he was learning some things—and that Davin was the one who was pushing him in that direction. And maybe he was pushing a little in return.

The next two days at practice both boys worked hard. Jared was starting to enjoy the way his body felt. He could run much farther and faster before the pain set in. And as Davin began to run more seriously, Jared enjoyed the competition.

They would run their breakdowns at less than all-out speed, but they would play cat-and-mouse games through the races, and then, at the end, one or the other would make his break. More often than not they finished very close together. When Davin won he would brag and tease, but then Jared would push all the harder to win the next one.

What Jared liked, though, was that they were pushing each other and both getting better. And on their bikes, after practice, they were extending themselves to get up the hill, even after tough workouts.

Maybe the best thing was that Jared was less concerned about his big brother's reputation and about his dad's hopes. He was simply enjoying track and wanted to do well for his own sake.

On Thursday the boys were tired after another double breakdown, which they had run faster than ever before, but they still pumped up to the pond after practice.

At first they told each other they weren't going farther up the trail. They just wanted to stay in the shade. But after half an hour or so, Davin said, "We might as well ride up partway."

Jared was thinking the same thing. So Jared and Davin pumped up the first easy grade, going fairly slowly, and then they made it to the switchback, geared down, and went to work on the long, steep climb up the front of the mountain.

Jared really didn't want to go too far, but he was leading today, and he told himself he wasn't quitting until Davin did. He knew Davin was playing the same game.

After a few minutes sweat ran into Jared's eyes and dripped off his nose. His lungs were heaving as he opened his mouth wide and tried to drink in enough air. He knew he had already put too much strain on his legs for one day. His calves were knotting up painfully and the tops of his thighs were burning and stiffening, beginning to shut down.

He geared down to his lowest gear, and the pedals

whizzed around with little resistance. That meant the progress was agonizingly slow, but he didn't want to quit. Finally, without looking back, he gasped, "You had enough?"

"Not me, white boy."

Jared's anger flashed. Why wouldn't he just drop that stuff? Things went so well when they just competed, pushed each other along. Now Davin had to ruin a good time and make Jared feel awkward and uncomfortable again. Jared drove harder, extending his lead over Davin to twenty yards.

The path was very rocky at that point. Jared felt his back wheel slip a couple of times, and in his exhaustion he found it hard to keep control of his bike. But he wanted to wear Davin down, force him to quit.

"Check it out," Davin yelled from behind. "The white boy thinks he's *bad*."

Suddenly Jared had had enough. He grabbed his hand brakes. In one quick motion, he dropped his bike to the side, stepped away from it, and turned around. Davin had his head down and was pumping straight at him.

"Davin, I'm *sick* of your mouth," Jared shouted, and he grabbed for Davin's handlebars.

Davin's head popped up, and in his surprise he veered to the right. But he was thrown off-balance, and his bike went down.

Words were still spilling from Jared's mouth—anger that continued from its own momentum—even as Jared watched Davin strike the ground, hard. Jared heard the thud of Davin's shoulder, and saw his head smack the ground, the rocks. He saw Davin grab his head with both hands and curl forward. But he didn't realize how serious it was until he dropped on his knees and saw the blood oozing between Davin's fingers.

"Are you okay?" Jared asked, not wanting to accept what he was seeing. The bike was still between Davin's legs, and Jared pulled it away. Then he knelt closer to Davin.

Davin was moaning, sort of crying, but he didn't speak. His breath was wheezy and coming in desperate bursts.

"Davin . . . uh . . ." Jared knew he had to think, but he was just kneeling there, staring at the blood dripping from Davin's fingers. Davin's eyes were open, but Jared knew he wasn't seeing anything. "Davin. *Davin!*"

Then Davin's body slumped, his hands falling away from his head. The blood was running off his hair and into the dirt.

"*Davin!* Can you hear me?"

Jared felt the panic well up in him. He tried to think what he was supposed to do. He had had some first-aid training in Boy Scouts, but nothing came to him. He slipped his hand under Davin's head and held the wound away from the dirt. He knew he had to do something.

But he couldn't move.

Davin's eyes were blank.

Seconds were ticking by, and Jared seemed locked where he was. "Davin. Davin," he kept calling.

Then Davin stirred and blinked, and his eyes finally focused in on Jared. But he looked confused.

"Davin, I'm sorry. I knocked you down. You hit your head."

Suddenly Jared knew what he had to do. He set Davin's head down, jumped up, and pulled the duffel bag loose from the back of his bike. He had worn an extra T-shirt on the way to practice, when the air was still cool.

"What?" Davin mumbled, as though he couldn't formulate his question.

"I'm sorry. I lost my temper and pushed you," Jared said. "You were knocked out for a minute. You cut your head. But don't worry. We'll put pressure on it." He tore the shirt down one side and began twisting it into one long bandage. Then he dropped down again. "Let go for a second, Davin," he said. Davin was gripping his head again.

Davin let his fingers loose and raised his head a little. Blood and dirt were matted in his hair. When he tried to sit up, blood trickled down his neck. Jared wrapped the shirt around twice, pulled it fairly tight, and then tied it off. Within seconds the red was oozing through the white T-shirt. Still, Jared was pretty sure he had done the right thing. But what should he do next?

"What happened?" Davin asked. He sounded only half conscious.

"You . . . fell off your bike, Davin. It's okay. You cut your head, and you were knocked out. But you're okay now."

Jared was scared by the confusion that lingered in Davin's eyes. Maybe he was hurt badly. Maybe his skull was cracked. Jared had to get him off the mountain somehow, and he wasn't sure how to do that. Or he needed to get help to Davin—up on the mountain—and he didn't know how to do that either.

He had to make the right decision. And he had to do it fast. "What do I do?" he found himself whispering. But he told Davin, "Don't worry. Everything's okay. Just rest for a minute."

"What happened?" Davin asked again.

"Davin, I'm sorry. It was my fault."

But Davin didn't seem to understand.

Chapter 8

Jared tried to consider all his options. He knew that Davin couldn't ride a bike, and he didn't think it would be good for him to hike down the trail. He might lose too much blood. And the heat couldn't be good for him.

"Davin, stay here and rest. I'll ride down the mountain and get help up here as fast as—"

"No. Don't leave me." Davin's eyes had lost that filmy, unfocused look, but they had begun to dart about, as though he were desperately taking everything in, trying to make sense of what he was seeing. "What happened to me?" he asked again.

"Davin, don't you remember? We were riding up the mountain. You . . . fell over on your bike. You hit your head."

"Don't leave me. I want to go home."

"I know." Jared tried to think. Maybe he couldn't leave Davin. He was just too scared and confused. "Okay. You can't ride your bike. We'll have to walk. We'll cut straight down. It's kind of steep, but it won't take as long."

Jared was not sure Davin could manage a long walk. Maybe he could sort of slide down to the next switchback. If they got that far, and Jared had to run for it, at least Davin would be closer. At the same time, he hated to leave his bike, in case he needed it to go for help.

But he had to do something, and getting Davin off the mountain as fast as possible seemed the only answer now. So he helped Davin to his feet and gripped him around the waist. The two of them made their way straight down the mountain, sometimes just scooting on their backsides. The mountain was steep, and rocks and brush got in the way. Jared went ahead at times, forcing his way through the brush and then taking some of Davin's weight and almost carrying him through.

They made it to the next level of the trail rather quickly, but Jared could see that Davin was losing strength. His legs were wobbling. He was moaning with every breath.

Jared kept reassuring him in a soft voice. "You're okay, Davin. You're okay. We'll get you off this mountain."

Jared still wished he could convince Davin to sit down so that he could make a run for it. More than anything he wanted someone to help him—someone who knew what he was doing. But Davin clung to him as though his life depended on the contact.

Still, the hot sun threatened. Davin seemed a little more distant all the time, as though his consciousness were slipping away with his strength. Jared knew that Davin had to be in shock, and he remembered that a person in shock should lie down and put his feet up. But how could he do that now?

Jared thought of cutting straight down the mountain again, but the brush was thicker below the lower trail. Besides, the trail was the better way, since it angled toward the pond and the road they needed to get to.

So Jared got under Davin's arm and took all the weight he could. Staying with the trail, the two fell into a steady, slow pace. "Good, good," Jared kept saying. "You're doing great." He tried to get a look at the bandage. As far as he could tell, the bleeding was under control.

But Davin couldn't seem to understand what was happening to him. "What are you doing?" he mumbled. His speech was thickening.

"We're walking down the mountain. It's not too far. You can make it."

Jared could feel Davin leaning on him more all the time. The trail seemed ten times longer now, walking, than it ever had on their bikes.

But they kept trudging ahead. And Jared kept questioning himself. Maybe he was doing the worst thing he could. But they had come this far. It wasn't all that much farther to the pond, where maybe Jared could let Davin rest for a few minutes in the shade.

Then Davin came to a stop. "I'm sick," he said, and he began to slump. Jared twisted and caught Davin, held him from going down.

"Davin, we've got to keep walking. You just have to keep going a little longer."

"I can't," Davin said, and he sounded distant, as though he were fighting to stay awake.

Jared thought of trying to put Davin over his shoulder, in the fireman's carry, but he knew that wouldn't work. It wouldn't be good to have Davin's head hanging down.

"Davin, listen to me," he said. He was still struggling to hold him up. "I'm going to carry you piggyback. It isn't too far. I can do it. But you've got to help me."

"I can't," Davin said, and suddenly he twisted and his body wrenched. Jared heard a splat in the dirt and knew that Davin had vomited.

That meant something. Jared remembered that it wasn't good. A concussion. What was he supposed to do for a concussion? But he didn't know. All he knew was that he didn't dare leave him here on the trail.

"I'm sick," Davin mumbled again, but Jared thought he felt him take a little more of his own weight. So Jared held Davin's arms high, twisted under them so that his back was to Davin, and then he pulled Davin's arms down over his shoulders. "Okay. Hold on, and I'll reach down and get your legs."

Davin said something Jared couldn't understand. Then Jared bent and grasped Davin's legs, but he couldn't get a good enough grip to lift him. Davin was a little taller, and it was hard to reach low enough. But Jared tried again, and this time he bent his knees more and got under him a little better. When he came up this time he was able to hold on to Davin's legs, at the back of his knees. Once he had him up he shifted him a little and then leaned well forward so that Davin didn't have to do much holding.

The problem was that Davin's weight was dead on Jared's back, and they were heading downhill. Jared took some careful, tentative steps and then set out at a pretty good pace. He figured it had to be one shot. He couldn't stop and put Davin down. He'd never get him up again.

So Jared strode forward, taking secure but long steps, and letting gravity pull him down the hill. He was already tired, but he told himself he had no choice. This wasn't a decision, like whether to stop pumping up the hill. It was just something he had to do.

He drove his legs forward, counting the steps, thinking that maybe two hundred would do it. He could hold out for two hundred steps, he told himself. But by the time he made fifty, he didn't think he could even do a hundred.

All the same, he kept going—striding out, counting. Sixty-eight, sixty-nine, seventy, seventy-one. "Davin, are you okay?" Seventy-three, seventy-four. "Davin, say something if you can hear me." Seventy-six, seventy-seven.

Davin only groaned, and Jared had no idea whether he was responding.

Jared was scared. All this time he had wondered what was best, but he hadn't had time to think what a mistake could mean. Suddenly it hit him. Was Davin bleeding badly again? Was the bandage still in place? Was he sapping Davin's strength away when he should be letting him rest? Maybe he should have followed his first thought and taken his bike and gone for help. Was he just making things worse, putting Davin in more serious danger?

He had lost the count. But he knew he had to be close to one hundred, and there was no way he had come halfway. He was probably still two hundred steps away.

He couldn't do it.

He knew he would have to stop, soon, and then go for help. But he could go a few more steps. His back was breaking, it seemed, and his legs were throbbing with pain. His breath was coming in gasps. Sweat was dripping off his nose and chin. But he kept taking steps.

A little farther. I can make it a little farther, he kept telling himself. A few more steps.

He made it to the point where the trail turned suddenly left and straight at the pond. But the land was almost level from this point. The gravity wasn't there to help him anymore.

Make it to the trees, he told himself. And now he was saying out loud, "Step, step, step." But he was staggering, and his knees weren't working right.

Suddenly they gave way. He didn't let himself fall hard. He let his knees hit, and then he reached with his hands and took the brunt of the fall. He was careful not to twist so that when his chest hit the ground, Davin was cushioned on top of him. Still, Davin moaned as he felt the jar. "Don't," he said. "Don't."

Jared's face was in the dirt. He had banged his cheek fairly hard. But his desperation was to get more air. Davin's weight was pressing down on him.

He twisted a little and drew in long breaths. His whole body was shaking, his legs jerking in spasms.

Jared couldn't think what to do. He just had to breathe and rest. And yet, at the same time, he knew he couldn't let Davin roll off his back. Maybe he could get back up somehow, with Davin still in position; but he would never be able to pick him up the way he had before.

And so Jared breathed and let his muscles rest. Davin moaned but said nothing. "Davin, can you hear me?" Jared kept asking. But he got no response.

Jared didn't know what it meant. Maybe Davin was in serious trouble. Maybe Jared was letting too much time go by. He pushed up with his arms, got himself on his hands and knees, with Davin still on top. Then he raised up slowly, agonizingly, his back cramping with pain. At the same time, he grabbed Davin's arms, desperately trying to hold him straight.

Jared waited on his knees and took a couple of long breaths, and then he made the supreme effort. He lifted himself enough to put one foot in place. He remained bent forward, and then, with one great surge, he got the other foot under him. He stumbled and almost went down, but managed to find his balance and then hoist Davin up enough to grab his legs.

Again Jared stayed bent over to keep Davin from slipping, and started ahead. His back couldn't take much of this, and his knees were already threatening to give way again. But Jared knew he had to make it at least to the trees, the shade.

"I'll make it to the pond," he told Davin, who was now moaning with every step.

"Step. Step. Step," Jared kept telling himself. Each word brought out a grunt, like the sound shot-putters make when they release the shot.

He couldn't really see ahead, but he watched where his feet came down and tried to keep his balance square.

A few more. A few more, he repeated, not aloud now, but inside his head.

He was falling forward, and he would have crashed onto his face had he not let his knees give way again. But this time he couldn't hold Davin straight. He hit on his side, and Davin rolled off his back. Davin groaned and reached for his head.

"I'm sorry. I'm sorry," Jared said, already scrambling up on wobbly legs. He grabbed Davin under the arms and pulled him the last several yards into the shade.

Should he put his legs up? Wouldn't that make his head bleed all the more? Jared didn't know.

He just didn't know.

He hardly realized that he was crying. "Davin, Davin, can you hear me?"

Davin didn't respond, and for the first time Jared let the panic take him. "Davin. I'm sorry. I'm sorry. Davin. *Davin!*"

Davin moaned, and it seemed a response. Jared told himself to think, to act. He checked the bandage, and it was secure. He could let Davin rest. Then what? He could never get him on his back again, not unless Davin could stand, and he was showing no sign of being able to do that.

Jared knew he had to get help. If Davin woke up and found no one with him, he might panic. But if he didn't get help, Jared didn't know what might happen.

Still, he hesitated. "Davin, I'm going to run for help now. I'll be back as fast as I can. Just rest. Don't give up. I'll hurry. Davin, can you hear me?"

But Davin didn't move, didn't even moan.

"Davin. Don't give up. You can't give up. I'll get help as fast as I can."

Jared took off running. For thirty meters he sprinted all-out. He felt light, not having Davin on his back. But then the weakness and pain hit him like a club. His legs slowed. He felt as though he were heading down the straightaway in the four hundred, except that he had four or five four-hundreds to run—maybe more.

But he pushed, drove his arms, dug for all the strength he could find. His legs would only move so fast, but he concentrated on lifting his knees, thrusting his arms—everything the coach had told him.

He was heading downhill again now, and only the gravity kept him running. He knew where the first house was, and he concentrated on that.

By the time he hit the paved street he was barely running, but now the house was only another hundred meters, and so he tried to kick, to pick up his speed. He managed it for a few strides before his legs almost stopped.

But he didn't quit, didn't walk. He kept pushing for that front door. When he got there he slapped at the doorbell, missed, slapped again, and then dropped to his knees. No one was coming. He hit the doorbell again, held on to it. And now he could hear someone.

When the door opened, a woman looked down at him, obviously shocked. "A boy's hurt," he gasped. "Call nine-one-one."

"What?"

"A boy. Up by the pond." Jared inhaled, with a quick, desperate gasp. "Call an ambulance. His head's bleeding. He's gone unconscious."

"All right," the woman said, and dashed away.

Jared dropped his head into his hands. He rolled onto his side and tried to get air—but suddenly he thought of Davin. He jerked himself back to his knees. He had to get back to Davin.

He yelled through the open door, "Send help straight up the trail to the pond. I'm going back."

He struggled to his feet, stepped off the porch, and started to run again—this time uphill. He only made it across the street before his legs refused. But he walked as hard as he could, staggering as he went. Tears were running down his cheeks.

And the same thought kept running through his mind: What if he had killed his friend?

C h a p t e r   9

Jared was sitting with his dad in the waiting room outside the emergency room at the McKay-Dee Medical Center in Ogden. Jared had a few scratches and bruises. A doctor had cleaned up and bandaged the bad scrape on his right cheek. He was also dehydrated, but the doctor told his father to keep getting liquids into him and he wouldn't need intravenous feeding.

The two were waiting now because Jared didn't want to leave until he knew how Davin was. He had asked the paramedics in the ambulance, but they hadn't told him much. They had gotten to the mountain quickly, even before Jared could make it all the way back to Davin, and they had acted fast—checking Davin, getting an IV going, applying a better compress on the wound.

They had worked on Jared too. He had collapsed once he knew Davin had help. And he still didn't remember the ambulance ride to the hospital very clearly.

At the hospital Jared had called home. No one

had answered, so he had called his dad's office at the university, across the street from the hospital. His dad had come right over. When his dad had arrived, Jared had told him the whole story . . . almost. But he couldn't get himself to admit that he had knocked Davin off his bike. He told his dad the same thing he had told the paramedics and the doctor: Davin had fallen.

After an hour or so, Mrs. Carter came out to the waiting room and said not to worry, that Davin was doing all right. The head cut wasn't as serious as it looked. "He lost some blood, but there's no fracture," she said. "He does seem to have a concussion. They're doing a CAT scan to see how serious it is. But the doctor says all the signs are good. He's not in any danger." She smiled with those big dimples.

"I didn't know what to do," Jared said. "I thought maybe I should let him rest up there while I ran for help."

"The doctor said it's better you didn't leave him," Mrs. Carter said. "He might have hurt himself. Or he might have just wandered off and got lost. He wouldn't have known what he was doing. He still doesn't know how he got to the hospital."

"You mean, he doesn't remember any of that stuff—how we got down and everything?"

"No. He keeps asking us what happened. He doesn't remember. I told him you hiked down with him, but he doesn't know anything about that."

Jared hadn't told her about carrying him.

"Could he have brain damage or anything like that?" Jared asked.

"The doctor doesn't think so." She patted him on the shoulder. "Don't worry," she said. "You did the right thing. The doctor said that the bandage you tied on him was exactly right."

Jared nodded. He was feeling better. He took a drink of water from the cup he was holding, and he was finally able to swallow easily.

"How did you hurt your cheek?" Mrs. Carter asked.

"I fell down," was all Jared said.

"Well, I can tell you did everything you could to help him. I hope you know how much I appreciate it." Tears came into her eyes, and Jared realized that she was probably more worried than she was letting on.

But Jared's chest was loosening for the first time since he had seen the blood oozing between Davin's fingers.

When Mrs. Carter went back into the emergency room, Mr. Olsen patted Jared on the back and said gently, "I'm proud of you, son."

But Jared didn't want that. He felt the numbing vibrations in his muscles, the exhaustion finally sinking all the way in as the fear loosened its grip; but still, a tightness stretched across his forehead. He had the feeling that something—his own guilt—had grabbed his temples and would never let go. He still didn't want to leave, not until they had the results of the CAT scan.

Another half hour went by, and this time Mr. Carter came out. He was wearing a dark suit, but he had loosened his tie, and he didn't look his usual crisp self. He also looked more concerned than Mrs. Carter had. Jared wondered whether something had gone wrong.

"I can't get anyone to tell me how much longer Davin will have to stay," Mr. Carter said. "If the CAT scan is okay, they said we could take him home. But that might take a while longer. Why don't you go ahead and go home?"

"Yes, I think we should," Mr. Olsen said. He looked at Jared. "You need to get some rest too."

When Jared stood he found that his calves were knotted up. When he tried to take a step, his foot slapped flat on the ground. He almost stumbled.

But he wasn't concerned so much about that. What he wanted to know was what Mr. Carter was thinking. He looked stern, and he hadn't said anything about Jared helping Davin. Maybe Mrs. Carter had made things sound better than they really were.

Jared and his dad walked out through the glass doors of the emergency entrance. Jared was moving slowly, and Mr. Carter walked alongside him, as though he were escorting him, the way a friend walks another friend to the door. But once outside, he said, "Jared, I'd like to know what you boys were doing up there on the mountain."

"We were riding our bikes up a trail."

"Yes, I know that. But hadn't you just come from a heavy workout on the track?"

"Yes."

"So what possessed you to ride up a mountain at a time like that? Davin's legs had to be tired before he ever started."

Jared heard the accusation in Mr. Carter's voice.

The grip on his forehead tightened. "We've been going up there almost every day," he said softly. "We thought it would get us in better shape."

"Well, you could just about bet that something like this was going to happen," Mr. Carter said. "You ride up there with your legs tired—on a rocky trail. That doesn't make a lot of sense. Not if you boys are serious about track."

Mr. Olsen said, "Apparently the boys thought they were going the extra mile."

Mr. Carter ignored Mr. Olsen. He drilled Jared with his hard-set eyes. "It just doesn't make sense," he said again, and he didn't hold back the anger in his voice.

Jared nodded.

Then Mr. Olsen said, "Jared, it really wasn't very wise. I hope you boys know better now." His voice sounded weak and apologetic.

Everyone was silent. Mr. Carter had his hands on his hips now, and he was looking away from Jared.

"I'm sorry," Jared said, finally.

Mr. Olsen added, "Phil, we both feel bad about this. Jared worked very hard to get your son down off the mountain, but it would have been better if—"

"I'm just glad it wasn't any worse," Mr. Carter said, and maybe some of the anger was gone.

Jared took a breath of relief and asked, "Did the doctor say how long he'll have to miss track?"

"No. We haven't asked about that yet. But don't worry, he'll be back."

Jared thought he knew what Mr. Carter meant, and he couldn't believe it. Jared didn't aim to get any advantage out of this. Did Mr. Carter think this was all a way to get Davin out of competition with Jared? Now it would be even harder for Jared to tell what had really happened—how Davin had really fallen.

"Would it be all right if I come over after a while—when Davin gets home?" he asked.

Mr. Carter turned back toward the doors. "I don't think so. He needs to rest."

"Okay. I'll come over tomorrow."

Mr. Carter didn't answer. He was walking away. But that's when Mr. Olsen said, "Say, Phil."

Mr. Carter stopped and looked around.

"I guess you got back from your trip sooner than you expected. I was just thinking, if Davin feels well enough, that offer is still good to come over this weekend." He hesitated, got no response, and then added, "Of course, if Davin isn't ready by then, we could put it off until next week."

Mr. Carter stood and stared. The anger in his eyes seemed to build until he looked as though he might raise a fist and knock Mr. Olsen down. Jared had an impulse to jump between them.

Finally, in a low, hard whisper, Mr. Carter said, "You don't get it, do you, Dennis?"

"What?"

"You don't take the hint very well, do you?"

Mr. Olsen's hands came up, palms spread wide, as if to say, again, "What?" But he couldn't seem to come up with any words.

"I'm not coming to your house—not this weekend, not ever. It's been all I can do to be cordial with you. I thought I could manage it, but I can't. There's no one on this earth I'd rather *not* have dinner with. And I would think that you would know that. I would

94

think you might have hung your head in shame when you saw me instead of starting all this 'old buddy' talk."

"Phil, I don't know what you mean. I thought we *were* friends. As far as I'm concerned, we *are* friends."

Mr. Carter laughed. "You're just as phony now as you ever were, Dennis."

Mr. Olsen seemed stunned. Jared turned to walk away, to get away from the embarrassment, but his dad wouldn't leave it alone. "Phil, I don't want this to happen. I know there was some awkwardness between us—during our senior year—but remember all those years before that. We were *good* friends."

"Dennis, I remember *all* of it. You only remember the parts you want to."

"Well, I don't know. Maybe. But I'd like to be friends now. And I'd like our sons to be friends."

Mr. Carter laughed. The anger was gone, but the hatred wasn't. "Dennis, let me tell you what I've told my son. I told him *never* to trust your boy—or anyone else who's white. That's the most important thing he needs to understand if he's going to survive in this country."

Mr. Olsen seemed stunned. "Phil, I don't understand that. Why did you move to Wasatch if you don't want your son to be around whites?"

"I didn't say anything about being 'around' whites. He's going to be around them—with them, by them—all his life. He just can't start thinking he's *one of them*. When he makes that mistake he'll get kicked in the teeth, the same as I did."

Mr. Carter stepped a little closer. "I grew up where

white people said I had to live—on the wrong side of town. And I grew up thinking that all those people in their fancy houses up on the hillside were better than I was. But my kids aren't going to think that way. They live way up on that mountain where they can look down and say, 'We're as good—or better—than anyone around here.' They may have to go to an all-white school, but that's not so bad either. They might as well know who it is they're competing with."

"Come on, Phil. I grew up just as poor as you did. We're not in any kind of competition with each other."

"But that's where you're wrong, Dennis. I've been in competition with you—and the rest of you Ogden High white boys—all my life. And guess what? I won. I beat you guys at your own game. I hope you look up at my house now and say to yourself, 'That colored boy whipped me—just like he used to do on the track.'"

Mr. Olsen shook his head and said, "Phil, I had no idea you felt that way."

"Don't give me that. Not now. When I was a kid I was stupid enough to play along with that phony act of yours. But you opened my eyes—and they've stayed open ever since. I don't want you in my house—and I'm not coming to yours." Mr. Carter turned toward Jared and pointed his finger at him. "You stay away too. I don't want you and Davin to have anything to do with each other."

Jared stared at the hand—the gold rings, the pointing finger—and somehow it seemed unreal. *All* this seemed unreal. Jared wanted to get away, to go home, and believe that things this ugly, this angry, couldn't really happen. People—adults—should never act this way. And no one should accuse his dad—*his dad*—of anything so . . . wrong . . . or mean . . . or . . .

"Phil, for crying out loud," Mr. Olsen said, "can't we talk about this?"

But Mr. Carter was walking away, and this time he kept going.

Mr. Olsen stood there for several seconds as Mr. Carter disappeared into the emergency room. Finally he looked at Jared. "Son, I don't understand what's going on," he said. "I treated him like a friend when most white guys wouldn't—and you can't imagine the abuse I took for that. I guess it did get harder as we got older. But things were just a lot different back then."

Jared didn't like what he heard in his dad's voice. So much weakness. Somehow Mr. Carter had seemed easier to believe. But Jared really didn't want to know what his dad had done to make the man so angry. He was ashamed just to think about it.

"Jared, I don't care what Phil says. You and Davin can be friends."

But his dad didn't know. He didn't know what a mess Jared had made of things.

Jared didn't try to put his feelings into words, but what he sensed was that he and his dad were somehow partners in all that was wrong. Both of them were guilty. Both of them had hurt their friends. And there seemed no way to make anything right, ever again. Jared's forehead was ready to burst.

Chapter 10

All the way home, Mr. Olsen never stopped talking. Over and over he claimed that he had been a good friend to Phil Carter, but Jared thought he sounded as though he were trying to convince himself. What did it mean to be a friend "to" someone anyway?

Jared said nothing. He went to his bedroom and tried to rest. But he couldn't sleep—partly because he ached so badly, and partly because his mind wouldn't shut off. He wanted to talk to Davin, and now Mr. Carter was saying that he couldn't. Jared wondered whether Davin would remember what had caused him to fall, and if he didn't, whether Jared should tell him.

At dinner that evening everyone was actually home. Kent was working at a Gas 'n' Go, and his schedule changed all the time. Lately, Jared hadn't seen him much. Lori worked at a Burger King in Ogden. A lot of evenings lately she had been at work.

Tonight, though, everyone was together, and they

all wanted to hear about Jared's "adventure," as Lori called it. But it was his dad who told most of the story.

"So did you actually save his life?" Lori asked. "Are you like this big hero now?"

Lori looked like her mother, with almost-blond hair and a sprinkling of barely noticeable freckles. She also had her mother's way of smiling—glancing sideways, her top lip sliding up a little at a time. But Lori's smile showed lots of metal these days, and she was more of a tease than her mom was.

Jared didn't bother to answer. In fact, he tried to change the subject. "Can someone go up and get our bikes off the mountain?"

Mrs. Olsen said, "Maybe your dad and I can walk up, after supper. We need the exercise."

But Mr. Olsen wouldn't let Lori's question die. "I don't know whether he saved Davin's life, since Davin probably never was in really serious danger. But Jared didn't know that. He put just the right kind of bandage on the wound. Then he got Davin up on his back, and he carried him down."

"Only part of the way," Jared said.

"But a *long* way. And then he ran to get help. The paramedic from the ambulance crew told me that when he first got there he was almost as worried about Jared as he was about Davin. He said Jared was dehydrated and suffering from heat exhaustion."

"So is that why you're moping around now?" Kent asked, picking up Lori's teasing tone.

Mrs. Olsen said, "Kids, leave him alone. He *is* tired."

"Something else peculiar happened that upset both of us," Mr. Olsen said.

Jared looked up and tried to let his dad know, with his eyes, that he didn't want to get into all this.

But his dad didn't seem to notice. "Mr. Carter was very upset about the whole thing. He didn't think the kids should have been up there in the first place. He ended up telling Jared he didn't want him to be friends with Davin anymore."

"After he carried him off the mountain? I don't believe it," Lori said. "What a jerk."

"He may not have known all that; anyway, there's a lot more to it," Mrs. Olsen said, and she glanced at Jared. "But let's leave things alone for now."

Kent looked at Jared and said, "So did Mr. Carter think going up there was your idea or something?"

"I don't know," Jared said, and he looked down at the chicken breast Mom had baked. He cut into it and tried to let everyone see that he just wanted to eat and be left alone.

For a time no one said anything. The family was sitting at the dining room table, which was in a little alcove off the kitchen. The afternoon light was very bright. Everyone was sitting in his and her usual places, the way they had for as long as Jared could remember. And yet, Jared had the strange feeling that everything was new, that life had changed in some way.

He hoped that things would somehow get back to normal. When the summer was over Nick would come back, and school would be sort of regular too, even if

it was junior high. Maybe then Jared wouldn't feel so
. . . but he didn't know what he felt.

Mrs. Olsen had asked to drop the subject, but
that was never Mr. Olsen's way. "I think Phil was
worried about his son," he said. "And he was upset. I
doubt he meant all of the things he said. But it be-
came pretty clear that he wasn't really upset with
Jared so much as he was with me. And I guess it all
goes way back."

"What do you mean?" Lori asked. "I thought you
were like best friends and everything."

"Well, we were—at one time. Up through about
sixth grade, we were together every day—at school,
around the neighborhood, all the time. When we got
older, we didn't spend as much time together, but we
were still friends."

"Why did you stop spending time together?" Lori
asked.

"Well—you know—in seventh grade we started
having school dances and all that sort of thing. In
those days, whites and blacks just never did things
like that together. I think the black kids had their
own dances—somewhere. I'm not sure. I just don't
remember them coming to the school dances."

"Didn't you ever ask him if he wanted to go?"

"Lori, it's hard for you to understand. Those are
good questions now, but we didn't even ask them
back then. I don't think Phil and I ever talked about
race. We just sort of pretended that it didn't exist.
But I don't think it ever occurred to us that we could
go out on a double date or something like that. In
high school I gave him a ride home after football

practice every day. And around school we still hung out together some."

"Maybe he felt like you white guys sort of shut him out," Kent said.

Dad nodded. "Yeah. I think he did. I think that's what he's talking about. And I wish I could do it over and handle some things a little differently. But I can't change the past. I was just hoping to do things right this time around."

That all sounded fair enough, but something in Jared told him that his dad wasn't telling everything. "Dad, did you *do* something to Mr. Carter?" he asked. "He's *so* mad at you."

Mr. Olsen set down his fork and leaned forward, with his arms on the table. He looked at his plate, not at Jared. "Something did happen once—something I've always felt bad about. But I'm not sure if that's what he's mad about or not."

Everyone waited.

Mr. Olsen spoke softly. "We won our league championship in football when we were seniors. After the game a player on the team—a guy named Gary Lawrence—invited everyone up to his place for a celebration. I'm sure Phil felt like he was invited. Gary knew that I was closer friends with Phil than anyone else, and so he came over to me and told me he didn't think his parents would want to have a 'colored' guy in their house."

"You've got to be kidding," Kent said.

"Look, I've tried to tell you, a lot of people were like that in those days. And a good many people probably still are, unfortunately. They just hide it more."

"Didn't you tell the guy what you thought of him?" Lori asked. She sounded disgusted.

"I don't remember," Mr. Olsen said quietly. "He kept saying he wouldn't mind, personally, but he knew his parents would. And I didn't want to embarrass anyone, so I just told Phil I didn't want to go, or something like that, and I gave him a ride home."

"He must have known what was going on," Mrs. Olsen said.

"Yeah. I'm sure he did. But I was too embarrassed to tell him the truth. And I think he was too embarrassed to say anything either. I guess I thought it was the best thing to do. But we drifted a lot further apart after that. So I suspect he did put the blame on me. And maybe he should have. But I still don't know what else I could have done. I was seventeen, and we were living in a different world from the one you kids know."

Jared wanted to believe all that. He wanted to believe that his dad had done his best and that Mr. Carter was the one making too much of the whole thing. But Jared had seen Mr. Carter's anger, and he had seen the pain in the man's eyes. Jared had a hard time believing that what he had just heard was the whole story.

Something was still gnawing at Jared, something he had felt when he had heard the two men talking to each other. "Dad, you don't treat him . . . *normal*," Jared said.

"What do you mean?"

"You're super nice, or something. I don't know."

Mr. Olsen was staring at Jared, looking confused. "I'm just trying to be friendly."

"He puts you down, Dad. He makes fun of you, and you just let him do it."

"Well, I—"

"Dad, it makes me think that you *know* you did something wrong."

The room had gotten very quiet. Mr. Olsen shrugged. "Jared, I told you what I did. There's nothing else that I know of."

Everyone was looking at Jared. "I'm not hungry," he said. He got up from the table and turned away.

"You go rest, honey," his mom told him. "You've been through a lot today."

The dining room was silent as Jared walked down the hallway to his bedroom. When he got there he lay down. He wanted to sleep and not think, but an image kept coming back to his mind. He kept seeing Mr. Carter's face, his eyes—the anger and pain. Those eyes sank deep into Jared and said, stronger than words, "Your dad's not telling the whole truth." And the image connected to a more intense, more immediate memory. He saw his own hands reaching for Davin's handlebars. He heard Davin's bicycle crashing onto the ground, saw his head bounce off the rock.

He never translated the images into words, never made any resolution as to what he should do. But he was left with a sick feeling of shame—both for himself and for his father.

The next morning Jared didn't go to track practice. His body ached, and he was so tired he couldn't seem to wake up. His mom told him to go ahead and sleep.

When he finally did get up, his legs and back hurt so badly that he had trouble walking. But he was hungry. He hobbled into the kitchen and found some cereal. Mrs. Olsen came in while he was getting some milk out of the refrigerator. "Hi," she said. "How are you feeling?"

"Okay."

"We got the bikes," she said. "We took Davin's to his house, and we talked to Mrs. Carter for a minute. She said Davin was doing fine."

Jared didn't want to get back to what they had been talking about the night before, so he asked, "What are you doing today?"

"I've been trying to put together lesson plans for this teacher-prep class I'm directing later this summer."

Jared nodded. He was pouring the milk on his cereal.

"Jared, when I saw Mrs. Carter, I realized that I had met her before."

Jared nodded.

"She's a nice woman."

Jared nodded again. He was trying to think of something else to talk about.

"I spoke at this women's book club a few months ago, and she was there. I didn't really think about it again until I saw her."

"Do you think the coach will be mad at me for missing track?"

"No, I don't think so. If I were you, though, I'd call him and tell him what happened."

Jared carried his bowl of cereal to the table. He had put in a little too much milk, so he had to walk slowly. When he sat down, his mom sat down across from him. The sun was on her face, and she didn't have any makeup on. She looked sort of transparent. She reached across and patted Jared's hand. "Jared, Mrs. Carter likes to read books, and so do I. She had some interesting things to say that day, and I thought I did too. She was nice, and I try to be nice. That's *all* that counts. We just need to forget all the rest. If you and Davin enjoy each other, that's the only thing that counts."

"Mr. Carter won't let us be friends."

"Well, I'll tell you something. But don't ever tell anyone I told you this." She laughed. She had a quiet but hissy way of laughing that always sounded sort of strange, even though Jared had heard it all his life.

"What?"

"Parents can tell their kids all kinds of things, but they can't live their kids' lives for them. If you and Davin want to be friends, there's really not much Mr. Carter can do about it. He can keep you apart at times, maybe, but he can't keep you from seeing each other at track—and this fall at school—and if you're friends, you're friends."

"You don't know Mr. Carter, Mom. When he tells Davin to do something, Davin *does* it."

"Well, maybe. Outwardly. But if Davin likes you, he likes you. And that's that."

"I don't know if he does, Mom."

"Really?"

"Yeah. One minute he seems to like me, and the next minute he's giving me a hard time—making stupid jokes about my being white. It's like he only wants to point out the differences between us. Like he doesn't want a friend."

"Does that bother you?"

Jared thought for a minute. He wanted to tell her the rest of it, tell her what he had done. But he just couldn't. "Sure," he said. "But when the summer is over, Nick will be back. It's not like I *have* to be friends with Davin."

"Well, maybe what you two went through together yesterday will break down some walls between you. Maybe he'll feel different about some of those things."

But Mrs. Olsen didn't know the whole story. And Jared couldn't bring himself to tell her.

"You know, one of the women in that book club told me something interesting. She said that some of the neighbors weren't all that excited about a black family moving into the neighborhood. But when they got to know Mrs. Carter, they liked her. A lot of these people have never been around blacks. But when they met a *person*—instead of some idea they had in their heads—their feelings changed. I think that's how this whole racial thing has to end—just one friendship at a time."

Jared nodded. He did like that idea. But he knew something else. "Mom, some people would rather keep their idea than have a friend."

"I know," she said. She nodded, and surprisingly, her eyes filled with tears. "Honey, that's an amazingly wise thing for you to notice. You're growing up, you know that?"

Jared thought maybe that was true. But he wasn't certain how he felt about it. Lots of things were becoming more complicated than he had ever imagined they would be.

On Monday, when Jared went back to track practice, Davin wasn't there. The coach told everyone that Davin's doctor had told Davin he would have to miss at least a week of practice.

All the next week Jared heard nothing from Davin. Jared had thought he might call, but he didn't, and Jared didn't dare call the Carters' house.

Jared worked out every day, but he didn't ride up the mountain. He was tired, and he didn't really want to go by himself. When he ran at practice, his legs felt heavy and slow.

On the following Monday Davin came back. He still had a little patch on his head, covering the cut, but he said he could run. He took things easy though, not doing all the training runs, and not going very hard when he did. He seemed a little quieter too, and Jared didn't know how to read that.

Jared tried to act normally, but it was hard. He didn't know how the two of them stood, and Davin wouldn't say much to give Jared any lead. When practice was over, Jared walked over to Davin, who was changing his shoes. "I guess you don't want to ride up just as far as the pond?" he asked.

"I can't. My dad would kill me."

"Okay." But Jared heard more than the words. He heard the distance, the coldness in Davin's voice. Maybe he had remembered what happened on the mountain. "Davin, I've been thinking about the day you got hurt. I'm sorry it happened. I just—"

"Look, we never should have gone up there after running so hard. My dad's right about that."

"Yeah. I guess."

Davin got up. "Well, I'll see you," he said, and he started to walk away.

"Davin, do you want to come over to my house for a while?"

Davin stopped and turned around. "I better not," he said.

"Won't your dad let you?"

Davin's eyes slid to the side. He spoke softly. "Look Jared, it's just not worth it. Let's just . . . leave things the way they are."

And he walked away.

Jared got his bike and pedaled home. He told himself that the injury hadn't turned out to be all that serious, so he didn't have to feel guilty. And he told himself that he didn't care about Davin anyway. But he felt some sense of loss that he didn't understand—and he felt very lonely.

Chapter 11

For two weeks nothing changed between Davin and Jared. There was a meet that first Saturday, but Davin said he wasn't ready to run. He was still getting his strength back.

That was probably true. But when the runners had done breakdowns, Davin, after the first couple of days, was hanging right in there with Jared. And before long Davin was beating Jared as often as not. In fact, he seemed to be trying harder than he ever had. Jared ran the four hundred in the meet, but he didn't feel good, right from the beginning. He finished fourth after running in second most of the way.

During the next week Davin talked to Jared once in a while, and at times seemed quite friendly. But he pushed the competition between them harder than ever. "Don't get your hopes up," he told Jared one day. "Because you're *never* going to beat me again." Then he watched Jared and waited for a response.

Jared didn't say anything.

But Davin wouldn't let it go. "Come on, Jared.

Tell the truth. You want to get me this next time, don't you?"

"Lay off, Davin."

"Just say it. Do you think you can beat me or don't you?"

"No, Davin, I don't have a chance against you," Jared said sarcastically, and he stepped onto the track and began his cool-down jog. He could hear Davin laughing.

J. C. Cotler was standing nearby, and he laughed too. He and Davin had started hanging around together quite a bit now. That made no sense to Jared, since he knew that Davin didn't even like the guy. But then Jared wondered whether Davin really knew what he was doing right now.

All the same, there was nothing Jared could do about any of it. He looked forward to the end of the summer, and he tried to focus on his own running. Recently, especially after his poor showing in the last meet, he felt his dad and brother giving up on him. But as the two of them showed less interest, Jared found something to care about. His legs were beginning to snap again. As the area championships approached, he started to get excited. He had the feeling that he could beat any of the runners in northern Utah—including Davin—if he could have his best day of the season. Maybe he had no chance at the state championship, with all the Salt Lake City runners competing, but it would be nice to qualify and see what he could do.

So Jared pushed himself very hard. And Davin was pushing too. There was no mistaking anymore that they were racing against each other. The team had two more meets before the area championships. On Saturday the runners would be traveling south to Provo to run against some teams in Utah County. None of Jared's family would be able to go, and Jared was glad. He just wanted to run the race for himself, and he wanted to win it.

Coach Heywood rented a bus for this trip, and all the way to Provo, eighty miles, Jared was nervous. A lot of the runners were fooling around, but Jared had little to say. Davin's dad had agreed to travel with the team and help with the coaching for the day. So Davin sat quietly next to his dad, near the front of the bus. Jared was sure that Davin was going to go all out to win this time.

The meet was at the Timpview High School track, close to the mountains, like the Wasatch track. Jared got off the bus and warmed up by himself. He said nothing to Davin even when they ran together in the four-by-one-hundred relay. The team made almost perfect "sticks" and finished second, their best race of the year. But that didn't matter much to Jared. The real race was still coming up.

As Jared stood by the track and waited for the girls his age to finish, it was Davin who finally spoke. "Why do we do this?" he said. "It's like giving yourself the flu—on purpose."

Jared laughed nervously. He had thought the same thing, almost in the same words. "At least it's only the one-minute flu," he said.

"No. It's the twenty-four-hour flu, all pushed into one minute."

Both boys laughed again.

Mr. Carter was watching from across the track.

As soon as the girls finished he called Davin over. The two talked seriously, and then Davin walked over to get his starting blocks. Jared saw something that took him by surprise. He had seen that look before—that day up on the mountain. Davin was scared.

Jared turned around and looked up at the mountains. He tried to clear his mind and just get ready to run. But he knew what was going on. Today he was racing Mr. Carter, not just Davin, and he wanted to beat both of them. Jared still felt guilty about the fall Davin had taken, and for never having told anyone the truth. But he also knew the price he had paid to get Davin off the mountain. He told himself that his effort had evened things out, that he didn't have anything to apologize for. It was Davin—and Mr. Carter—who had turned this race into a grudge match. What he longed for was to drop all the bad feelings, but that wasn't going to happen now. So Jared vowed to show Davin what he could do.

When Jared stepped into his blocks, and as he came set, he vowed to run the race of his life. When the gun fired, he broke from the blocks harder than he ever had before.

Jared was in the second lane. Davin was outside, in the seventh. Jared could see Davin and most of the rest of the runners through the first curve.

The runner in lane five, a tall guy with long hair, was supposed to be the fastest. But Jared was holding his own with him, and he quickly made up ground on the runners in the third and fourth lanes. Jared was almost sure he was going out too fast, and so he held back a little, but he felt great, and he wanted to *go*.

He came out of the first curve in good shape, still

about even with the tall kid. But Jared could see Davin out in lane seven, really flying—maybe ahead of everyone.

Jared was tempted to open up even more, but he told himself, *Go too hard now, and you'll pay. Wait. Wait.*

Jared felt his spikes spring off the soft track. His legs felt light and powerful. Big Evan Garner was standing near the track, halfway down the backstretch, and Jared heard him bellow, "Go Davin! Go Jared! You've got 'em. Keep it up."

Jared did sense that the runner next to him was falling back a little more, and he had gained on the tall guy. But it didn't mean anything. Nothing was real until the pain came and his legs began to slow.

All the same, he was floating, feeling lean, feeling the power in his legs. His breath was coming harder, but his lungs weren't screaming, not yet.

He went into the second turn, taking those slightly crossed steps, driving toward the pain, but still feeling good. At the top of the curve the wind slowed and then after another few steps was gone. All was silent except for the yelling that was out there in the distance, not really part of him. And now the tunnel was coming, when the only things that existed were the white lines, the distant finish, and the pain. But the pain wasn't there. Still not there.

As Jared came out of the curve he didn't have to look to the side. He knew that he was a step ahead of the tall guy in lane five but that Davin was even with him, maybe a little ahead.

Jared could win this race. He suddenly drove

himself harder, told himself he had plenty left. As he did, his legs finally felt the strain. But not like before. He could push back against this wall. And even though his chest was tightening, there was no sickness.

So he drove himself down the straightaway and felt the tall guy slip back. Davin was still there, just a sense of movement and sound way out to his right. He knew the two of them were close, but he thought he had the lead. He could beat him.

Someone was screaming through the veil of numbness, "Jared, you've got it. You've got it. Bring it home. Bring it home."

Jared wanted it. But now the strain was building. His legs were beginning to thicken, his stride shortening no matter how hard he tried to drive his knees. The pain had waited, but it was there.

Maybe the tall guy could come back. Maybe Davin had more left. *No!* He wouldn't let that happen today.

The finish line was only twenty meters away. Jared drove his legs and arms, tried to get to the end of the pain. It was almost over.

And then a giant voice, heavy and deep, jammed into his head. *"Davin, don't let him beat you!"*

In the same instant, something went out of Jared. He broke. He managed to get to the finish line, but he felt the movement on the outside, felt Davin go by.

As he crossed the line he stumbled and went down to his knees. He gasped for air in violent jerks. The nausea hit him with such sudden power that he felt his stomach convulse. He choked and swallowed hard and kept most of the vomit from coming, but the acid burned his throat. He coughed and raised his head to spit out the bitterness.

He didn't care about the race. He just wanted to breathe, and then get to the grass.

But someone had him around the shoulders and was bending down next to him. "Great race," the voice said. Coach Heywood's voice. "You almost won it. You and Davin got first and second."

The coach helped him to his feet, and Jared was surprised how quickly his body was recovering. The nausea was gone, and his legs weren't as dead as he expected them to be.

That's when he spotted Davin. He was leaning against his dad, breathing hard, his head rolling back. He looked gray, and his legs didn't want to hold his weight. Jared had the feeling that Davin had paid some higher price, that there was nothing left in him now.

Mr. Carter was talking fast. Jared heard him say that he was proud of Davin, but he couldn't hear the rest. Davin seemed not to care. He hardly seemed to be hearing.

"Boy, you hit the wall, didn't you?" Coach Heywood was saying to Jared. "You had him, and then your legs just gave way. All you have to do is get so you can drive it home now. You and Davin just might push each other all the way to the state championship. One of you two guys could get it. These were some good runners you beat today."

Once Jared was steady on his legs, Coach Heywood crossed the track to talk to Davin. Jared watched and kept thinking about that moment—

when he had quit. He remembered the voice—Mr. Carter's voice. What had he said?

Jared walked to the grass and lay down. He let the sun bake down on him, and he took big, smooth breaths. He felt the tingling, the sense of returned life, as his body got the oxygen it needed.

Then the sun disappeared, and Jared opened his eyes to see Davin standing over him. "Why did you let me win?" he demanded.

"What?"

"You heard me?"

"Hey . . . I didn't." Jared sat up.

"What's with you, Jared? You don't have to do me any favors. When I beat you, I'll beat you."

"Davin, I told you. I didn't let you win. I wouldn't do that."

"How come you always hold out longer than I do on our bikes? How come you have just as much left as I do at the end of a breakdown? And then, all of a sudden, you've got nothing left at the end of a race?"

"I don't know. I think I ran too hard in the beginning." But Jared was uneasy with his own answer.

"My dad told me not to trust you," Davin said with disgust. "And I don't."

Chapter 12

When Jared got home his mother wanted to know how he had done. She was thrilled when he said he had taken second in both races. But it didn't take her long to realize that something was wrong. "So how come you look so miserable? What's up?" she asked.

"Nothing." Jared really didn't want to talk.

"Is Davin still avoiding you?"

"Davin's mad at me."

"Why?"

"I don't know, Mom," Jared said, and his voice showed his irritation.

Mrs. Olsen left him alone after that. But later that afternoon his dad was more persistent. He had obviously talked to Mrs. Olsen and found out that something was wrong. When Jared wouldn't tell him what it was, he started another one of his little talks about the importance of Jared and Davin getting along with each other.

"Dad," Jared finally said, "Davin doesn't like me.

And I don't like him much either. That's all there is to it."

Kent and Lori were both working that night. Jared was sitting on the family room floor, eating a burrito and watching TV. His parents were sitting at the table nearby in the dining area.

"Well, it's not quite that simple," Mr. Olsen said.

"Dennis, maybe it is," Mrs. Olsen replied.

Mr. Olsen let out a long, audible breath, and Jared kept his eyes on the television set. He hoped that was the end. But his dad couldn't let it go. "Son, I hate to see you let this opportunity go by. I'd like to see you two kids make up for what went wrong between Phil and me."

"It doesn't work that way, Dennis," Mrs. Olsen said. "You know that."

Jared just kept looking away. He knew his dad was only pausing to think what else he wanted to say.

"Jared," Mr. Olsen said, "have you ever heard Martin Luther King's 'I have a dream' speech?"

"Sure."

"Well, every time I hear that I think about the way the world *ought* to be and how far we still have to go to make it that way. I hope you feel that way too. And I hope you'll try your hardest to make Davin welcome here."

Jared knew that something was wrong with what his dad was saying. But he didn't know how to say it. So he said, "Okay, Dad, I'll try," and then he got up and carried his plate to the kitchen sink. He rinsed it quickly and put it in the dishwasher. Then, without saying a word, he walked to his bedroom and shut the door.

"I'll make him welcome!" he said out loud. "I'll beat him next time—and shut his mouth forever."

On Monday morning at practice Jared watched Davin to see what he would do. But Davin came nowhere near Jared until the coach called everyone together.

Coach Heywood had all the athletes sit on the grass, and then he said, "You're coming along well, kids. But we need to keep working hard. We've got this little tune-up meet this week, and then next week—the first week of August—will be the area championships. One thing we've got to do is re-arrange the relays. We might as well stack one or two of them at each age level and try to get those qualified for the state meet."

He looked down at his clipboard and read off the changes he had made in the relays, starting with the older runners. When he came to the twelve-and-thirteen age group he said, "Our four by one hundred hasn't done very well. I think that's the one to drop. Morgan and Olsen, I'd like you to run the four by four hundred. That means two four-hundreds in one day for you, Jared, but I think you're ready to do that now."

Jared was stunned. His stomach rolled at the very thought of it. Two four-hundreds in one meet. He was sure he couldn't do it.

"Carter, I want you and Russell to run the two-hundred-meter legs in the medley relay."

Jared glanced at Davin, who looked troubled—or confused. Jared had expected him to be relieved.

When the meeting broke up, Jared stood. He was still feeling overwhelmed. The coach seemed to see his concern and walked over. "Jared," he said, "I know that sounds like a lot. But you're in good shape. You can handle it."

"Won't I do worse in both?"

"I don't think so. You'll—"

But just then Davin stepped up next to Jared. "What's going on?" he demanded, and he sounded angry.

Coach Heywood gave him a surprised look. "What do you mean?"

"Why'd you choose him?"

Coach Heywood lifted the baseball cap from his head and rubbed his hand across his damp forehead. "What are you talking about? Do *you* want to run two four-hundreds?"

"No. I just don't know why you picked him."

Jared couldn't believe this. "Hey, go ahead. You do it. Be my guest," he told Davin.

Davin spun toward him. "I could handle it just as well as you could."

Jared looked straight into Davin's eyes. "There's something *wrong* with you, Davin. Nothing ever satisfies you. Do you think I want to—"

"Wait a minute!" the coach barked at the two of them. "Just calm down. Listen to me." Both boys turned back toward him. "You two have been running about even. I thought about putting you both in the four by four hundred. But, Davin, you're still coming back from your injury. I just thought it might be too much for you."

"Yeah," Davin said, "and black guys don't have the guts to run two long races, right?"

The coach shook his head slowly. "Look, Davin, you can play that game with a white coach. But don't try it on me. I'll tell you what—you run that four by four. I'll put you down for it. That's probably better anyway."

"I didn't say I *wanted* to run it."

The coach laughed and shook his head again. "Davin, you don't know what you want."

"All I'm saying is—"

"You've said plenty. Plan on running two four-hundreds in the next meet. And I want to see what kind of guts you *do* have."

Coach Heywood turned then and called out for the team to jog a lap. "We're going to take some starts and do some sprints. No breakdown today."

He stepped away, and Davin and Jared were left standing next to each other. "I didn't say I wanted to run two four-hundreds," Davin mumbled again.

Jared almost laughed. His anger was gone, and now it struck him as funny that Davin had talked his way into the same mess he was in. "It's going to be tough," he said.

But Davin didn't like that. "Not for *you*!" he said. "You can just quit at the end—the way you did last time."

"I didn't quit."

"Don't give me that!" Davin grabbed Jared's shoulder and pulled him around so they were facing each other. Then he stabbed a finger into Jared's chest. "I know what you did!"

A lot of the runners on the team were close by, and everyone turned to see what was going on.

122

"You don't have any guts, Olsen." He pounded his finger hard against Jared's chest again. "You don't finish what you start."

"Shut up, Davin. You think—" But he stopped.

"I think what?"

Jared shook his head and stepped back.

"What do I think, Jared?" Davin almost jumped forward into Jared's face. "Tell me what I think, Jared! Say it!"

"Look, Davin, let's just—"

"No. You tell me. You had something you wanted to say to me." Davin punched his finger into Jared's chest one more time.

Jared had a sudden impulse to smack the guy in the face, or at least to push him back. But he couldn't let himself do that. He just couldn't. His anger had caused too much trouble before. "Davin, I didn't mean anything."

"Oh, man. You're so gutless. You—"

"Hey, lay off, Carter." Big Evan Garner stepped between the boys. "Just lay off."

"Stay out of this," Davin said, and he tried to step around Evan.

Evan grabbed both of Davin's shoulders and held him away. "How come you guys always have to start fights?" he demanded.

"*What* guys, Garner? What are you talking about?"

But Evan didn't answer. He just held Davin at arm's length. And by then the coach was coming. He ended things quickly.

Jared got away from everyone as quickly as he

could. He went off to jog his lap. But his anger was gone. He wished Evan had never stepped in, had never said anything like that. It only made things worse.

The rest of that week Jared and Davin ran together but not together. When the coach had them run breakdowns they went all out. They had never run harder in workouts, but they said next to nothing to each other.

Davin dropped an occasional insult, but Jared wouldn't bite. He just let it all go by, and the standoff continued. Jared rode his bike every day after practice, and gradually he had started heading up the mountain again. He didn't try to go very far, but he wanted to stay in shape for biking. He had already made up his mind that once track season was over he was going to make it to the top. It was something to do—something to tell Nick when he got back. And maybe something he would tell Davin.

And then, one day, coming down the trail, he met Davin coming up. It was a big surprise. When they met, neither knew what to say. The trail was too narrow to pass by each other easily. Each had to get off his bike and carry it by.

"I didn't think you were doing this anymore," Jared said.

"That's what my dad thinks too," Davin answered. He didn't sound hostile.

"Do you think it's good for our legs—when we have to run two four-hundreds this week?"

Davin took a long look at Jared, as though he had

something he wanted to say. But then he only said, "I don't know," and got back on his bike.

Jared was left with a strange feeling. Davin's voice had sounded sad, as though his words really meant, "I don't know anything." Jared really wanted to hate the guy—or to like him. But Davin was a moving target, and Jared could never quite take aim at him.

Jared came very close to turning around and following Davin. Maybe it would be a way to end all the bad feelings. But he didn't know how Davin would take that. Besides, when he thought about the next race, he knew he didn't want to feel good about the guy. He was going to beat him this time, and not have to listen to any more of his accusations.

And that's how Jared felt on the morning of the meet. He wasn't as angry as he had been, and he was nervous about having to run two four-hundreds, but he promised himself he wouldn't let up this time, especially knowing that Kent and his dad would be there.

The meet was at the Wasatch field, with two teams from nearby towns, Roy and Bountiful. In the early events the Wasatch runners did better than usual. Jared knew that his team was improving, but he could also see that the talent was thin on the other teams. Maybe that meant some of the pressure was off. He could go all out on the open four-hundred, and maybe he wouldn't be too pressed on the relay.

As he warmed up he didn't feel quite as strong and fresh as he had the week before. But as he stretched and ran a little, his legs loosened. He hoped they would have the spring he needed when the time came.

Mr. Carter walked down to the starting area, as usual. Jared saw him talk to Davin. He even heard him say something about improving his time. Davin was listening, and he looked serious and resolved, but when he walked away, carrying his blocks to the track, he passed by Jared.

"Good luck," Davin said.

Jared hardly knew what to think about that. He heard no sarcasm in Davin's tone. "Yeah. Good luck," Jared said, but he tried not to let himself lose his focus.

"Go hard, Jared!" he heard Kent yelling, but he didn't look up at him. He got into his blocks and waited, and when he heard the gun fire, he released himself into the race.

He came out feeling a little sluggish, but about twenty strides out he knew the power was there. He was in the sixth lane, and Davin was inside of him, in lane three. Jared had no idea how Davin was doing as they ran the first turn, but he had smoked the two guys outside him. He was running by himself.

He strode down the backstretch, feeling fine and light. His breath was coming steady and deep, was not labored. He had never thought that running could be a sort of pleasure, but he felt it now—the long, smooth strides, the sense that he was barely touching the track, and the energy within him telling him that he was in better shape than he had ever thought possible.

He was going fast—faster than ever before—as he

entered the second curve. No one else was on the track, it seemed. No one was fast enough to catch him today. His legs were springing, his knees lifting. He was breathing harder now, but the pain wasn't there.

He floated out of the corner, and that's when he suddenly realized that Davin was right with him. There were four lanes between them, but the two of them were the whole race. Everyone else was way behind.

Down the stretch they came, both running all out. Jared felt his legs begin to lose something, but he was not fighting, not breaking down. He was running hard, and he had the feeling that Davin would soon drop away. No one could take him today.

But Davin was staying tough, driving, holding his own.

The pain finally hit his body with twenty meters to go. Jared reached for another gear. He drove his arms harder, tried to accelerate through the finish.

The pain was real, as powerful as ever, but it wasn't frightening anymore. It was something to take on and beat.

He drove his arms, his knees, exerted everything he had, and then threw his upper body forward as he crossed the finish. Davin had never lost a step. The two crossed together.

Jared trotted ahead and then stopped and grabbed his knees. He stood, looking at the track, gasping for air. But he didn't let himself drop to the track. He was all right. He took a quick glance at Davin, who looked up at the same moment.

Davin gave a nod but said nothing. "Good race," Jared gasped.

Then Jared's dad showed up out of nowhere and grabbed Jared. "I think you won!" he shouted.

Jared wondered. He didn't know. He looked over at the finish line. A little huddle had formed. The timers and judges were all talking to one another.

Then he heard Mr. Carter's voice. "Davin, you still haven't learned to dig down. You have more speed than he does. You just don't *want* it badly enough."

Davin twisted away from his father and stepped back to face him. "No!" he shouted. He took a couple of deep breaths, and then he said, low and hard, "I gave it *everything* I had. But that's not good enough for you. Nothing is *ever* good enough for you!"

"Davin, that's nonsense. All I expect is—"

But Davin had spun around and was heading away. He trotted to the infield, where he grabbed his duffel bag. He jerked his track spikes off, dropped them in the bag, then sat down and started putting on his cross-trainers.

Mr. Olsen said to Jared, "I don't think that's fair. Davin ran hard. Both of you did."

Mr. Carter was walking toward Davin. But Davin pulled his shoes on and didn't bother to lace them. He got up and walked away. Mr. Carter said, "Davin, come back here."

But Davin didn't stop. He walked, and then trotted, toward the stadium gate.

"Davin, don't you do this!" Mr. Carter yelled. "You come back here!"

But Davin kept going, and finally Mr. Carter came

to a stop. Jared thought about the relay, the second four-hundred they were supposed to run. Was Davin quitting the team?

Suddenly Jared was running too. He ran to his own duffel bag and pulled off his spikes. Then he grabbed his other shoes and ran for the gate in his stocking feet.

"Jared, you have that relay to run," his dad yelled after him.

Jared knew that. But he kept running. When he got outside, Davin was gone. But Jared was pretty sure he knew where he would be. So he put on his shoes, grabbed his bike, and headed for the pond.

Chapter 13

Jared did find Davin at the pond. He had dropped his bike near the trail and then walked to the edge of the water and sat down. He seemed unsurprised that Jared would show up, but he didn't turn around.

Jared wasn't sure now what he intended to do. He put his bike down and walked closer, but he didn't say anything.

Davin allowed the silence for a time. But finally, without glancing back, he said, "If you think you're going to talk me into going back to run the relay, you might as well take off."

"I don't care if you run the relay."

Suddenly Davin twisted around. "Then what do you want?"

"I don't know. Nothing, I guess."

Davin looked back at the water. Jared let a little time go by, then sat down on a rock a few feet away. But he didn't say anything. He watched a couple of water striders darting about on the still water at the edge of the pond.

Jared let ten minutes pass, and Davin hardly moved. It was a standoff, as though both were waiting for the other to speak. And yet, Davin didn't tell Jared to get lost, and Jared was pretty sure that meant something. Finally Jared took a chance. "We ran a good race today," he said.

Davin didn't respond. He picked up a couple of little rocks and flipped one of them. It plopped in the water and sent a series of little waves in concentric circles. One of the water striders made a quick dart away, setting off its own flow of tiny circles.

"I don't know about you," Jared said, "but that's the best I've felt. That's the first time I've finished without wishing I'd never have to run another four-hundred."

"Then go back and run one. Enjoy yourself."

"Yeah, well, I didn't exactly *enjoy* it." He laughed quietly.

Davin flipped another rock in the water and then scratched up some more from the dirt near his feet.

"All I'm saying," Jared said, "is that the work we've done is paying off."

Davin suddenly threw the whole handful of gravel into the water. The rocks hit the surface like a little storm, making pockmarks everywhere, stirring up waves in all directions. "Look, Jared, lay off, okay? I'm quitting track. I'm quitting sports. And I'm going to tell my dad to get off my back and *stay* off. I don't really care what he or anyone else thinks of me any-more."

"In some ways I feel the same. I'm tired of trying to be as good as my big brother."

"Don't give me that. You don't have any idea what my life is like."

"I'm just saying that—"

"Jared, listen to me. I'm never, *ever* going to know—not for one second—what it's like to be a *normal* guy. And you know why?" He looked into Jared's face, his eyes as steady as rocks. "Because in this country—especially this town—normal will always mean *white*."

"That's not true, Davin. That's just something—"

"Don't tell me that, Jared. I know. Maybe some black guys can forget that stuff, but not me. My dad won't ever let me." Davin got up. He seemed unsure where he was going for a moment. But then he walked over and picked up his bike. Jared stood. He wanted to say something to keep Davin from going, but he couldn't think what.

Davin lifted his bike and started to turn around. But then he stopped and turned back. He stepped on the pedal and swung his leg over. He took a few strokes, geared down, and then started pumping hard—up the mountain.

"Davin, *don't!*" Jared yelled. "Your legs are too tired."

For a moment he told himself he would wait for Davin to take out his frustration. Then, when he came back, maybe he would be willing to talk. But Davin was pushing up the hill, bent forward in that bright red track suit, looking determined. Jared knew he couldn't let him ride by himself.

Jared got his bike and started up the hill. He didn't try to catch up. Davin was driving himself much harder than Jared wanted to, and Jared figured Davin would give up before long.

But Davin kept pushing past the first big switchback, and then all the way up the long trail that rose across the face of the mountain. When he made the second switchback, still with good momentum, Jared began to realize that Davin might be determined enough to make it today.

Jared was hurting. He had no real desire to do this, and his body was demanding that he stop. But Davin had geared down low, and he was grinding, grinding. In the stillness Jared could hear Davin breathing in raspy bursts, and he could see the bike lurch across the rocks.

Jared thought of the blood he had seen on the trail before, and he knew he ought to stop Davin. But he also knew Davin wouldn't listen. Jared just had to stay with him—if he could.

Jared almost quit at least a dozen times before Davin made the third switchback. But when Davin turned, he glanced down, just as Jared took a quick look up. The look in Davin's eyes said, "I'm going to the top today," and Jared suddenly wanted to do it too.

He stood up on the pedals and drove himself harder around the turn. He was gaining just a little now, and he felt a surge of strength.

By the time he caught up with Davin, Jared's second wind was gone. But they were not that far from the last turn.

Davin kept driving. Jared could see that he was wobbling at times, and he was almost crying in his own agony to get enough air. Jared knew he was taking too big a chance. But they were so close.

And then Davin's back tire came off a rock and slid sideways. The bike almost tipped over, and Davin had to put a foot down to catch himself.

With a gush of relief, Jared let go and put his own foot down. He was dropping forward on the handlebars to suck in air when he saw Davin right the bike and get his foot back into the stirrup.

"Don't stop," he growled. "Let's make it!" He pulled his weight up and stepped down on the pedal again. "Come on, Jared. Let's do it."

For maybe five full seconds Jared thought he couldn't go on. But then he placed his right foot back on the pedal, rose up with all his strength, and went after it again. "Let's do it," he answered, and put his head down and pumped with all his power. The pedals were spinning, and the progress was slow, but now Davin had invited him along.

They made the fourth turn. What followed was something Jared hadn't remembered. The trail leveled quickly after this last turn. Once they got around the switchback and a few yards beyond, they had essentially crested the mountain. There was only a slight rise from there.

Davin let out a little cry of relief and shifted up a gear or two. Jared did the same. They began to pick up speed. The rest of the ride was nothing. They pushed ahead to a point where the trail stopped. The top of the mountain was actually a large open area. It was hard to say where the peak was.

It didn't matter. They were on top.

Davin dropped his bike and stepped away just far

enough to collapse in the dry grass and weeds. Jared did the same, a few yards back. But he wasn't quite as tired as he expected to be. A surge of joy had come to him when he realized they had done it. And in only a minute or so he was getting up to look at the view below.

Davin got up soon after. "We weren't that far from making it before," he said in a gasp. "We just didn't know."

Jared nodded. He pulled his shirt out, wanting to wipe his face, but it was completely soaked with sweat. He kept taking long breaths, and he looked out across the valley. The Great Salt Lake spread out in the distance. The sky met the lake, and the two, both silver-blue, seemed to blend. Closer, by the mountain, he could see the high school—the track and the runners. It seemed strange that the world was going on as usual even though he and Davin had left it behind.

Jared felt a sudden pang of guilt. He really ought to be down there.

The two sat down and looked at the valley—and kept breathing. Jared was still numb, and his head seemed foggy, but he was amazingly happy.

Davin seemed a different person. "I *knew* I could do it today," he said. "At first I was mad, and then after that, it was like something I had to do. I hit that point back there when I slipped, and it seemed like I'd failed, and I just said, 'Man, no way. We're going to the top.'"

"I gave it up. I was glad to stop. Then I had to start all over when you took off again. I didn't think I could do it."

"Well, we did."

They let themselves breathe again. Jared was starting to feel that tingling, satisfying sensation that always came after the great effort was over. But his legs were throbbing, his calves even cramping. He was dripping with sweat. A little breeze was moving the air, though, and it felt good.

After a couple of minutes Davin spoke in that gentler voice he used sometimes. "Jared, I don't get you. I really don't get you."

"What do you mean?"

"I went back to the doctor yesterday—the one who took care of me at the emergency room. He wanted to check me after two weeks."

Jared didn't see the connection. He waited.

"He told me that when they brought you and me in, he thought we had both been hurt. He said you were as bad off as I was."

"Not really. I was just tired."

"He said you were dehydrated and stuff—because you carried me off the mountain."

"Just part of the way. It wasn't like—"

"No one told me that before, Jared. I asked my mom about it, and she said she thought you just helped me walk down. I think maybe the doctor might have said something to my dad, but no one told me."

"I didn't know how bad off you were. I had to do something," Jared said. But the guilt was there again. He ought to tell Davin the whole thing. It wasn't right to let Davin think he was a hero for carrying him.

"Wasn't it hard to get me down?"

136

"Yeah." Jared laughed. "A lot worse than a four-hundred."

But Davin took that seriously. "Really? A lot worse? Worse than this ride just now?"

"Yeah. But it was different. I got really scared."

"Scared? Why?"

"Well, I didn't know what was happening for sure." Jared hesitated, a little embarrassed. "I started to think you might be dying."

"Really?"

"Well . . . I didn't know."

Davin sat for a time and looked out toward the lake. Jared came close to telling him how the fall had happened in the first place, but he couldn't get himself to do it.

"I still don't get you," Davin finally said. "I mean, I appreciate what you did and everything, but you don't make sense to me."

"Why?"

Davin thought for a moment. But then he laughed. "For one thing, there must be something wrong with you, or you wouldn't be hanging around with a black guy."

Jared didn't laugh. "Davin, why do you always do that? People don't think that way."

"Oh, man. Here we go again. See, that's what I'm talking about. You're a good guy, Jared. You really are. But you don't want to see how things are. You'd rather lie."

The tone was back—that hostile, superior tone. Jared hated it. "You don't know that, Davin." He stood up, and he looked down on Davin. "You act like you know *everything* about me! But that's because you have your mind made up. You're the one who's prejudiced. You have been from the first."

Davin got up and faced Jared. "Jared, just once, for two minutes in a row, treat me like a regular guy—not your *black friend*—and we'll be cool. But you can't do that."

"No way, Davin. I try to treat you like anyone else. But you always bring up the stuff about being black. I don't *care* what color you are."

Davin laughed. He wiped his hand across his wet hair, then rubbed his hand on the front of his shirt. "If that's true, just tell me this. How come you let me win last week? What was that all about?"

"I didn't let you win that race because you're black." And finally Jared told himself the truth. "I let you win because of your dad."

"My dad?"

"He was over there screaming at you that you had to win. And all of a sudden, I . . . felt sorry for you. But it didn't have one thing to do with *him* being black or *you* being black. I just know what kind of pressure he puts on you all the time."

Davin looked down for a few seconds and seemed to think about that. Then he stared out at the valley. "My problem is, I don't ever know how to take anything. Those white judges said I beat you that one time, and I know I didn't. Maybe they messed up, like you said. But maybe they didn't want to hurt my feelings. I don't know." He dropped his head and looked down at the ground. "The coach puts you in the relay, and not me, and the last thing in the world I want to do is run two four-hundreds. But all I can think is that the coach is choosing you because you're white—even though he's black. It's the way I think. It's the way my dad has *taught* me to think."

"Maybe people aren't even thinking stuff like that most of the time."

"Yeah, maybe. But a lot of times they are. What was Evan thinking the other day? Tell me that? '*You guys* always start fights,' he tells me. So what was that supposed to mean?"

"He meant black guys. I know that."

"Okay. So where does he get that? Do black guys really start fights? I don't know. I don't know who I'm supposed to be."

"But most of the time you're the one who reminds me that you're black and I'm white. I'm not just some white guy either. Don't judge me by what Evan said. And maybe I do feel awkward sometimes, or don't know if something is right or wrong to say. Maybe I *shouldn't* care. I'll try, if you'll stop bringing it up all the time too."

"Okay. That's fair. But, Jared, from now on, run like you did today. Give me all you've got. And when I'm a jerk, you've gotta tell me I'm a jerk."

"Okay."

Jared wanted that to be the end, but the other thing was still there. "Davin, there's something else I've got to tell you."

"What?"

"I'm the one who made you fall that day—and hit your head." Jared swallowed hard. The words might cost him plenty, but he still felt relieved to have them out.

"What are you talking about?"

"Don't you remember anything that happened?"

"No."

"We were pushing each other, trying to see who could hold out the longest. And that was okay. But then you started calling me white boy, and stuff like that. I lost my temper. I stopped and got off my bike. You were coming at me, so I reached out to stop you. It threw you off balance, and you went down."

"No kidding?"

"Davin, I'm really sorry." Jared felt the shakiness in his voice, and he swallowed again. "I did carry you down, but I knew what happened was my fault. So don't make me out to be a big hero."

"No. That's not what I'm talking about. What were you going to do? Punch me out or something?"

"I don't know. I was just yelling at you to shut up, to stop saying that kind of stuff."

Davin laughed. "Hey, that's great. That's what you should have done."

Jared tried to laugh, but the relief left him on the edge of tears. "No. We could have talked about it. I didn't have to lose my temper."

Davin spoke softly when he said, "Jared, the doc told me you were *wasted* when they brought us in. He said you used every ounce of strength you had, carrying me, and then you *ran* to get me help—more than a mile each way. I know how that had to hurt. I just can't believe you could push yourself that hard."

"But I'm the one who got you hurt in the first place. I was just trying to make up for that."

"I don't see it that way. It just happened. You didn't *want* it to happen. But once it did, you paid the price. And you did it for me. I don't know if I could run that hard for someone else. I really don't know if I could push myself that hard for you."

"I think you would," Jared said.

Davin was still looking out at the valley. When he finally looked over, Jared wasn't prepared for what he saw. Tears had come into Davin's eyes.

And once Jared saw that, he couldn't hold back. Tears finally rolled onto his own cheeks.

Chapter 14

Jared and Davin coasted all the way down the hill and most of the way back to the high school stadium. By the time they got there the track meet was over and most people had already left.

Jared and Davin wanted to talk to Coach Heywood. They had made up their minds that they wanted to stay on the team, if he would let them.

They weren't ready for what they saw: Coach Heywood standing near the gate talking to Mr. Olsen and Mr. Carter. When the boys came riding toward them, all three turned around, and Jared knew that no one was happy.

"You boys missed the relay," Mr. Olsen said. He was holding Jared's duffel bag.

"We know."

"Jared, that's not something you do to your team."

Jared had no idea where to start any sort of explanation, so for now he said nothing.

Coach Heywood sounded a little gentler. "Do you boys *want* to be on the team?" he asked.

Both boys nodded, and then Davin said, "Yeah, if we still can be."

The coach tucked his hands into his back pockets. He looked from one boy to the other. "Well, I'll tell you," he finally said. "I have the feeling that both of you need to make up your minds that *you* want to run—whether your dads want you to run or not."

Jared watched the two fathers. Mr. Olsen looked down at the ground as though he were a little ashamed. But Mr. Carter looked right back at the coach. "If I push him, it's because he *needs* pushing," he said. "The boy has talent, but he doesn't *try*."

"He tried today."

"I don't buy that. He's capable of finishing stronger. But he's afraid it might hurt."

"Is that right, Davin?" Coach Heywood asked.

"I ran it as hard as I could." Davin looked straight in his father's eyes.

Mr. Carter obviously didn't like that. "Davin, let's go. We'll talk about this at home."

"I've got my bike, Dad," Davin said. "I'll—"

"We'll put your bike in the trunk. Now come with me."

"Dad, I want to ride down to Jared's."

"No." He looked at Mr. Olsen when he said, "Davin, I don't want you over there—not at all."

"Phil," Mr. Olsen said, but he sounded hesitant. *Careful*, Jared thought. "What can it hurt for the boys to be friends?"

Phil Carter turned toward Mr. Olsen, and he stepped closer. "Well, actually, Dennis, you could answer that question better than anyone. Why don't you tell my son how white kids treat their black 'friends'? Why don't you tell him how long that friendship is likely to last?"

Coach Heywood moved forward a little, as though he wanted to stop Mr. Carter from saying any more.

"Phil, okay. I guess you feel that I turned my back on you. But I—"

"You turned your back, all right."

"Look, I have the feeling that a lot of this goes back to that night we won the league championship in high school—and Gary Lawrence had that party."

"Oh. You have a *feeling* about that, do you?"

"Phil, I know I wasn't honest with you that night. I'll tell you what I told my family just the other night. I did the wrong thing. I admit that. But in those days, things were a lot different from the way they are now."

Mr. Carter shook his head, slowly, sadly. "Dennis, I've hated you for twenty-eight years. I've been pushing myself just so I could show you and Gary—and all the rest—that I was better than any of you. And that's your little summary of the whole thing? You were 'dishonest' with me. You 'admit' that. But then, that's okay, because times were 'different' then?"

"No. It wasn't okay. And I don't mean to make it sound trivial. But I didn't know what to do. Gary told me his parents wouldn't want you there—and I know that was terrible—but I didn't want to embarrass you."

Mr. Carter was still shaking his head. "I guess that's right," he said. "I guess that's how it would look to you. But there's no way you'll ever understand what you did to me that night."

144

"I think I do, Phil. It must have been—"

"No! You don't know, Dennis. Don't pretend you do."

The words seemed to tear from Mr. Carter's chest. The force somehow made them true. And Jared saw the shame in his father's eyes.

"You can never see it the way I did, Dennis. You just *can't*. It goes all the way back to grade school when all you white guys would have given anything to change places with me. I was the man. I could hit a ball farther, kick a football farther, run faster—anything. You know that, but you don't know what that did to me, do you?"

"No. I guess not."

"I knew the word nigger, but I thought it didn't apply to me. Because I was . . . *somebody*. I didn't want to have anything to do with black kids. I had *white* friends—and that was better."

Jared looked over at Davin. He seemed amazed. All this seemed to be new to him.

"I guess I knew what was happening by the time we hit junior high. But I didn't want to accept it. I just closed my eyes, no matter what happened. You still hung around with me some—and all the white kids still made a big deal out of me because I was the sports hero. But I was sinking into no-man's-land. I didn't have any black friends—and didn't want any. I didn't have any white friends either—not really— but I wouldn't admit that to myself."

"Phil, things were just so different then. I didn't have any idea that I was—"

"Don't give me that, Dennis." Mr. Carter suddenly stepped up close.

Coach Heywood reached out and grabbed his arm. "Come on, now. Listen to what the man has to say."

But Mr. Carter pulled his arm loose. "You can't get off that easily, Dennis. You played the part too well. You didn't say it out loud, but in a thousand ways you made me believe I could trust you. My mother used to tell me to be careful—to stay with my own. But I wouldn't listen. I just kept hanging on to the idea that I was better than other black kids. I was a football star. And I had white friends—or at least *one*, for sure."

Mr. Olsen nodded as if to say, "Okay. I see your point." But he said nothing.

"That night we won the championship, I was in my glory. I ran for two hundred yards, scored three touchdowns. Man, I was the *star*. People—white people—jumped all over me when the game was over. After, in the locker room, everyone was still coming up to me, slapping me on the back—all that stuff. Then Gary Lawrence walks in. 'We're having a party,' he says. 'Everyone's invited up to my house.' Do you have any idea what that meant to me? I had *never* been invited to anything like that. There had always been that line that I couldn't step over. And then, there it was. I was invited up to the rich kid's house. I was *accepted*. I could go to parties with the white guys."

"Okay. I understand better now." Jared saw his dad look at the ground again, embarrassed. "At the time, though, I wasn't even sure you knew what had happened."

"Hey, how stupid do you think I am?"

"Phil, I—"

"Actually, you've got a point. I *was* stupid. I turned to you like some kind of idiot, and I said, 'Should we go?' You said, 'Sure.' But I saw that look come into your eyes, like, 'Oh, man, maybe this won't work.' And then Gary gets you aside and the conversation starts. By the time you got back to me, you were whistling a different tune."

"Look, Phil, that's all true. But I was caught in a trap."

Jared's breath had caught in his chest. He wanted to believe in his dad, but why did his dad sound so weak and ashamed?

"Dennis, do you think I didn't know what was going on?" Phil demanded. "I played along with your little game that night because I didn't want to cause trouble. That's what black kids were taught to do in those days. I went home and sat in my bedroom, and I *cried*, man. I was seventeen years old, a big, tough guy, and I sat in my room and *cried*. It was the first time in my life I admitted to myself what I was. It turned out I was a *nigger* after all."

"Phil, there was nothing I could do. On my way to the shower Gary stopped me and said, 'Hey, maybe I shouldn't have said that.' Then he gave me this big story about it not bothering him if you came, but his parents would just about die. I argued with him, but he said I would have to make some excuse. So that's what I did. But at the time, it seemed like I was saving you a lot of embarrassment."

"Answer me one question, and by the way, I know the answer."

"What?"

"Did you drop me off and then go to the party?"

Mr. Olsen's eyes shifted down again. "Yes, I did, Phil. And I'm sorry about that. But I just didn't know what to do."

Mr. Carter nodded a couple of times. "Well, I'll tell you what you should have done. You should have told that redneck that if I wasn't welcome in his home, *you* didn't want to be there either. And then you should have invited people to *your* house. Or you and I should have gone somewhere, just the two of us. You could've done *anything* but turn your back on me—and that's what you did."

"Okay. Okay. You're right Phil. I was young, and it was a long time ago. But yes, that's what I should have done."

"It's not that easy, Dennis. All those other guys could say the same thing and I'd buy it. But they didn't have our history. You and I grew up together. And you let me believe that meant something. You're the worst kind of racist, Dennis. You want it both ways. You want to feel good about yourself, pat yourself on the back, tell yourself you aren't like the rest—but when the moment of truth comes, you bail out. And the worst part is, you're still playing the same game."

Mr. Olsen had no reply. Jared felt sick. He wished that his dad would at least say, "No. I was wrong then. But I'm not like that now." But he said nothing, and now Jared wanted to get away.

"Look," Coach Heywood said, "it's all out now. You've cleared the air. Maybe you can—"

"Hey—don't get me wrong," Mr. Carter said, and he laughed, with no joy. "I'm *glad* it happened. I

148

learned my lesson. It took me a while, but I turned tough." He glanced at his son. "So I owe you, Dennis. I owe you everything."

Mr. Olsen was quiet for a time. Finally he said, "Phil, I did let you down. And you're right—I've made excuses for myself all these years. But I guess I've always known that I was wrong. And I've felt guilty about it. Maybe that's why I've tried to teach my kids not to be prejudiced."

"Yeah, well, I've taken another approach. I've prepared my son for the worst. I don't want him to go through what I did. The last thing I want is to have my kids grow up thinking that they can trust whites—and then find out the truth."

The two stood looking at each other. Jared thought there was nothing more to say. But Coach Heywood was the one who spoke. "I doubt that teaching kids hatred is much of an answer."

Mr. Carter turned and looked at him.

"This man let you down a long time ago," the coach said. "Now he says he's sorry. It's up to you to decide what you want to do with that. But you're trying to pass your anger on to another generation. I don't see how that's going to get us anywhere. Maybe both these boys can learn from your mistakes."

"I'll decide that for myself," Mr. Carter said, but he was stepping back, retreating. "Davin, come on." He took Davin by the shoulder and turned to leave.

"Phil, I think you're wrong," Mr. Olsen said.

"What?" Mr. Carter turned back to face Jared's dad.

"You're right that I've been patting myself on the

back all of these years—and I shouldn't have. But I still tried harder than those other guys did, and I'm trying now. I want to do the right thing. And I want our kids to get past all the garbage that we had to live with."

Mr. Carter looked past Mr. Olsen, toward the mountains.

"Phil, I really am sorry."

Phil nodded. "Maybe so, Dennis. Maybe I ought to shake hands and say it's all forgotten. But it's just not that easy for me. I don't trust you. And I don't think I ever will. I'd rather just leave things the way they are."

But all the anger was gone from his voice.

Mr. Carter looked down at the boys. He looked sad, but he gave no hint as to what he was thinking.

But Davin seemed to sense something. "Dad, is it okay if I go down to Jared's?"

Mr. Carter didn't answer for a very long time. He stood as still as a statue. But finally he said, "I guess I'll leave that up to you."

Mr. Olsen was quick to say, "Phil, I think that's the right thing. Let's just—"

"Don't push it, Dennis," Mr. Carter said. "I don't want this. I'm still angry. And I've been angry for a long time. It's who I am, and as far as I can tell, it's who I'm always going to be. I'll let Davin choose for himself, but I fear for him. I fear what you and your son might do to him. My advice to him is to get in the car and go home with me right now."

Davin was standing by Jared, but he was looking at his dad. He seemed caught between. He turned to Jared and said, quietly, "I better go home."

150

He got his bike and walked toward the car. Mr. Carter glanced around at everyone, but he said nothing. He turned and followed his son.

"I'm sorry," Mr. Olsen said, and patted Jared on the shoulder.

Jared got his own bike and rode home.

His dad got there a little before he did, in the car. He wanted to talk things over with Jared, but Jared wasn't in the mood. He went to his room and lay on his bed. He didn't know what to do, but he knew what he wished. He wanted the world to start over. He wanted things to be right this time. He didn't want to deal with all the stuff that had happened before he was born; he just wanted to start fresh.

But he had to accept things the way they were. That's what Davin always said. He was bone tired—tired of thinking and tired of trying. He let himself drift off to sleep. But his mind wouldn't stop working, and he remained half-conscious, still upset.

An hour or so went by. Then he heard his door open. He was trying to open his eyes when he heard a voice.

"What are *you* so tired for?"

Jared sat up and looked at Davin, standing in his doorway. He was startled, partly from coming out of his sleep, but mostly from seeing Davin, for the first time, in his house.

"Some guys just can't take it. Run a four-hundred, bike up a mountain, and they're all wiped out."

Jared was still a little groggy, but he smiled. "We

have to run *two* four-hundreds next week," Jared said. "How are you going to do that?"

"Piece of cake," he said. "I'll beat you easy.

"Forget that. I—" But then something seemed to hit Davin. "Hey, who won the race today? Did anyone ever say?"

"My dad said that he thought I did, but I never heard what the judges decided."

"Well, it was close," Davin said, and he laughed. "But I'm pretty sure *I* won."

"Hey, I didn't want to say it, but I had you by at least a quarter of an inch. I looked over as we crossed the finish line."

"Yeah. And while you did that, I put on my big lean, and I got you. It wasn't that close."

"No way. And next week it won't be close at all. I'm going to beat you *bad*."

"Not a chance," Davin said. "I'm going to start *trying* now. You heard what my dad said. I didn't even try today."

"Oh, yeah. Right. I hate to say this Davin, but you're acting like a jerk."

"Hey, thanks. I was hoping you'd notice."

Both boys were still smiling, and to Jared, at least for the moment, it seemed as though the world were starting over.